'Meticulous, engaging. There's a refreshing honesty in what De Botton has to say' *Guardian*

'Moving' *Sunday Times*

'A complete delight' Amy Bloom

'Probes the very heart of marriage, its shifts and squalls, its great adventure, with such forensic tenderness. I laughed a lot, too' Deborah Moggach

'De Botton takes us through the stages of a marriage: misunderstandings and petty tiffs, acquiring of property, births of children, financial worries, occasional bouts of loneliness, dwindling of sex, the whole gamut of conjugal existence. Every note rings uncomfortably true . . . told with great wit and affection. He knows his stuff and the book builds into a truly wonderful and positive analysis of a successful lifelong partnership. It should be compulsory reading for anyone contemplating tying the knot' *Daily Mail*

'Shows off De Botton's ability to pin our hopes, methods and insecurities to the page . . . satisfying in conveying its particular truth. He pithily covers our continual need to re-establish that we're wanted, the dangers of sharing the contents of our sexual imagination and dozens of other subcategories' John Williams, *The New York Times*

'[I] read *The Course of Love* in two spellbound sittings. It's very beautiful and very important. You'll want to buy it for everyone' Derren Brown

'I loved it . . . a novel so sharp and real and economical and true . . . best of all, [it] made me feel incredibly happy about my marriage. And that's an amazing thing' Giles Coren

'Wonderfully acute, graceful and beautifully written. It will make me live differently' Susie Boyt

'Dazzling, positively eerie in its insights. You may find that the voice of Alain de Botton continues to comment wryly and incisively on your own private life long after you have finished *The Course of Love*. Give it to your children' Niall Ferguson

ABOUT THE AUTHOR

Alain de Botton was born in Zurich, Switzerland, in 1969. He has written over fifteen books spanning both fiction and non-fiction and is a bestselling author in thirty countries. His thoughtful and pioneering works, on subjects that range from religion to art, from our working lives to how we travel and spend our leisure time, have been described as a philosophy of everyday life. He also founded and runs The School of Life, a London-based organization dedicated to a new vision of education.

Alain de Botton's first book, the bestselling novel *Essays in Love*, was published when he was just twenty-three years old. Over two decades later, Alain returns to fiction and to the love story with *The Course of Love*.

THE COURSE OF LOVE

Alain de Botton

PENGUIN BOOKS

PENGUIN BOOKS

UK | USA | Canada | Ireland | Australia
India | New Zealand | South Africa

Penguin Books is part of the Penguin Random House group of companies
whose addresses can be found at global.penguinrandomhouse.com.

First published by Hamish Hamilton 2016
Published in Penguin Books 2017

011

Copyright © Alain de Botton, 2016

The moral right of the author has been asserted

Set in Fournier MT Std
Typeset by Jouve (UK), Milton Keynes
Printed in Great Britain by Clays Ltd, St Ives plc

A CIP catalogue record for this book is available from the British Library

ISBN: 978–0–241–96213–8

For John Armstrong,
mentor, colleague, friend

CONTENTS

CHILDREN

ADULTERY

BEYOND ROMANTICISM

ROMANTICISM

Infatuations

The hotel is on a rocky outcrop, half an hour east of Málaga. It has been designed for families and inadvertently reveals, especially at mealtimes, the challenges of being part of one. Rabih Khan is fifteen and on holiday with his father and stepmother. The atmosphere among them is sombre and the conversation halting. It has been three years since Rabih's mother died. A buffet is laid out every day on a terrace overlooking the pool. Occasionally, his stepmother remarks on the paella or the wind, which has been blowing intensely from the south. She is originally from Gloucestershire and likes to garden.

A marriage doesn't begin with a proposal, or even an initial meeting. It begins far earlier, when the idea of love is born, and more specifically the dream of a soulmate.

Rabih first sees the girl by the water slide. She is about a year younger than him, with chestnut hair cut short like a boy's, olive skin and slender limbs. She is wearing a striped sailor top, blue shorts and a pair of lemon-yellow flip-flops. There's a thin leather band around her right wrist. She glances over at him, pulls what may be a half-hearted smile and rearranges herself on her deck-chair. For the next few hours, she looks pensively out to sea, listening to her Walkman and, at intervals, biting her nails. Her parents are on either side of her, her mother paging through a copy of *Elle* and her father reading a Len Deighton novel in French. As Rabih will later find out from the guest book, she is from Clermont-Ferrand and is called Alice Saure.

He has never felt anything remotely like this before. The sensation overwhelms him from the first. It isn't dependent on words – which they will never exchange. It is as if he has in some way always known her, as if she holds out an answer to his very existence and, especially, to a zone of confused pain inside him. Over the coming days, he observes her from a distance around the hotel: at breakfast in a white dress with a floral hem, fetching a yoghurt and a peach from the buffet; on the tennis court, apologizing to the coach for her backhand with touching politeness in heavily accented English; and on an (apparently) solitary walk around the perimeter of the golf course, stopping to look at cacti and hibiscus.

It may come very fast, this certainty that another human being is a soulmate. We needn't have spoken with them; we may not even know their name. Objective knowledge doesn't come into it. What matters instead is intuition: a spontaneous feeling that seems all the more accurate and worthy of respect because it bypasses the normal processes of reason.

The infatuation crystallizes around a range of elements: a flip-flop hanging nonchalantly off a foot; a paperback of Hermann Hesse's *Siddhartha* lying on a towel next to the suncream; well-defined eyebrows; a distracted manner when answering her parents; and a way of resting her cheek in her palm while taking small mouthfuls of chocolate mousse at the evening buffet.

Instinctively, he teases out an entire personality from the details. Looking up at the revolving wooden blades of the ceiling fan in his room, in his mind Rabih writes the story of his life with her. She will be melancholy and street-smart. She will confide in him and laugh at the hypocrisy of others. She will sometimes be anxious about parties and around other girls at school, symptoms of a sensitive and profound personality. She'll have been lonely, and will never until now have taken anyone into her full confidence. They'll sit on her bed playfully enlacing their fingers. She, too, won't ever have imagined that such a bond could be possible between two people.

Then, one morning, without warning, she is gone and a Dutch couple with two small boys are sitting at her table. She and her parents left the hotel at dawn to catch the Air France flight home, the manager explains.

The whole incident is negligible. They are never to meet again. He tells no one. She is wholly untouched by his ruminations. Yet if the story begins here, it is because – though so much about Rabih will alter and mature over the years – his understanding of love will for decades retain precisely the structure it first assumed at the Hotel Casa Al Sur in the summer of his sixteenth year. He will continue to trust in the possibility of rapid, wholehearted understanding and empathy between two human beings and in the chance of a definitive end to loneliness.

He will experience similarly bittersweet longings for other lost soulmates spotted on buses, in the aisles of supermarkets and in the reading rooms of libraries. He will have precisely the same feeling at the age of twenty, during a semester of study in Manhattan, about a woman seated to his left on the northbound C train, and at twenty-five in the architectural office in Berlin where he is doing work experience, and at twenty-nine on a flight between

Paris and London after a brief conversation over the English Channel with a woman named Chloe: the feeling of having happened upon a long-lost missing part of his own self.

For the Romantic, it is only the briefest of steps from a glimpse of a stranger to the formulation of a majestic and substantial conclusion: that he or she may constitute a comprehensive answer to the unspoken questions of existence.

The intensity may seem trivial, humorous even, yet this reverence for instinct is not a minor planet within the cosmology of relationships. It is the underlying central sun around which contemporary ideals of love revolve.

The Romantic faith must always have existed, but only in the past few centuries has it been judged anything more than an illness; only recently has the search for a soulmate been allowed to take on the status of something close to the purpose of life. An idealism previously directed at gods and spirits has been rerouted towards human subjects – an ostensibly generous gesture nevertheless freighted with forbidding and brittle consequences, since it is no simple thing for any human being to honour over a lifetime the perfections he or she might have hinted at to an imaginative observer in the street, the office or the adjoining aeroplane seat.

It will take Rabih many years and frequent essays in love to reach a few different conclusions, to recognize that the very things he once considered romantic – wordless intuitions, instantaneous longings, a trust in soulmates – are what stand in the way of learning how to sustain relationships. He will conclude that love can endure only when one is unfaithful to its beguiling opening ambitions; and that for his relationships to work he will need to give up on the feelings that got him into them in the first place. He will need to learn that love is a skill rather than an enthusiasm.

The Sacred Start

In the early days of their marriage, and indeed for many years thereafter, it is always the same question for Rabih and his wife: 'How did you two meet?' – usually accompanied by an air of playful, vicarious excitement. The couple then typically look at one another (sometimes a little shyly, when the whole table has stopped to listen) to determine who should tell it this time. Depending on the audience, they may play it for wit or for tenderness. It can be condensed into a line or fill a chapter.

The start receives such disproportionate attention because it isn't deemed to be just one phase among many; for the Romantic, it contains in concentrated form everything significant about love as a whole. Which is why in so many love stories there is simply nothing else for the narrator to do with a couple after they have triumphed over a range of initial obstacles other than to consign them to an ill-defined contented future – or kill them off. What we typically call love is only the start of love.

It is peculiar, Rabih and his wife observe, how seldom they are asked about what has happened to them since they met, as if the real story of their relationship doesn't belong to an area of legitimate or fruitful curiosity. Never have they publicly fielded the one question that truly preoccupies them: 'What is it like to have been married for a while?'

The stories of relationships maintained over decades, without obvious calamity or bliss, remain — fascinatingly and worryingly — the exceptions among the narratives we dare to tell ourselves about love's progress.

It happens like this, the start that gets too much attention: Rabih is thirty-one and resident in a city that he hardly knows or understands. He used to live in London, but recently moved to Edinburgh for work. His former architectural practice shed half its staff after the unexpected loss of a contract, and redundancy forced him to cast his professional net wider than he would have liked — which eventually led him to accept a job with a Scottish urban design studio specializing in plazas and road junctions.

He has been single for a few years, since the failure of a relationship with a graphic designer. He has joined a local health club and signed up to a dating website. He has been to the opening of a gallery exhibiting Celtic artefacts. He has attended a stream of events loosely connected to his work. All in vain. A few times he has felt an intellectual connection with a woman, but no physical one — or the other way around. Or worse still, a glimmer of hope and then the mention of a partner, usually standing on the other side of the room, wearing a prison warden's expression.

Still, Rabih doesn't give up. He is a Romantic. And eventually, after many empty Sundays, it happens at last, almost as he has been taught — largely by art — to expect that it will.

The roundabout is on the A720 heading south from central Edinburgh, connecting the main road to a cul-de-sac of executive homes facing a golf course and a pond — a commission which Rabih takes on less out of interest than because of the obligations that come with his modest ranking in his company's pecking order.

On the client's side, the supervisory role is initially assigned to a senior member of the City Council's surveying team, but the day before the project is due to start the man suffers a bereavement and a more junior colleague is moved across to take his place.

They shake hands at the construction site on an overcast morning in early June, a little after eleven. Kirsten McLelland is wearing a fluorescent jacket, a hard hat and a pair of heavy rubber-soled boots. Rabih Khan can't hear anything much of what she is saying – not only because of the repetitive shudder of a nearby hydraulic compressor, but also because, as he will come to discover, Kirsten often talks rather softly, in the voice of her native Inverness that has a habit of trailing off before sentences are entirely complete, as though she has halfway through discovered some objection to what she has been saying or has simply moved on to other priorities.

Despite her apparel (or in truth partly because of it), Rabih at once notes in Kirsten a range of traits, psychological and physical, to whose appeal he is susceptible. He observes her unruffled, amused way of responding to the patronizing attitudes of the muscular twelve-man construction crew; the diligence with which she checks off the various items on the schedule; her confident disregard for the norms of fashion and the individuality implied by the slight irregularity in her upper front teeth.

Once the meeting with the crew is finished, client and contractor go and sit together on a nearby bench to sort through the contracts. But within a few minutes it begins to pour and, as there is no room to do paperwork in the site office, Kirsten suggests they walk to the high street and find a café.

On the way there, beneath her umbrella, they fall into a

conversation about hiking. Kirsten tells Rabih that she tries to get away from the city as often as possible. Not long ago, in fact, she went up to Loch Carraigean, where, pitching her tent in an isolated pine forest, she felt an extraordinary sense of peace and perspective in being so far away from other people and all the distractions and frenzy of urban life. Yes, she was up there on her own, she answers; he has an image of her under canvas, unlacing her boots. When they reach the high street, there is no café in sight, so they take refuge instead in the Taj Mahal, a sombre and deserted Indian restaurant where they order tea and (at the owner's urging) a plate of poppadoms. Fortified, they make their way through the forms, concluding that it will be best to call in the cement mixer only in the third week and have the paving stones delivered the week after.

Rabih examines Kirsten with a forensic focus, while trying for discretion. He notes light freckles across her cheeks; a curious mixture of assertiveness and reserve in her expression; thick, shoulder-length auburn hair pushed to one side; and a habit of beginning sentences with a brisk 'Here's a thing . . .'

In the midst of this practical conversation, he manages nonetheless to catch the occasional glimpse of a more private side. To his question about her parents, Kirsten answers, with a note of awkwardness in her voice, that she was brought up in Inverness by her mother alone, her father having lost interest in family life early on. 'It wasn't an ideal start to make me hopeful about people,' she says with a wry smile (he realizes it's the left upper front tooth that is at a bit of an angle). 'Maybe that's why the thought of "happily ever after" has never really been my thing.'

The remark is hardly off-putting for Rabih, who reminds himself of the maxim that cynics are merely idealists with unusually high standards.

Through the wide windows of the Taj Mahal, he can see

fast-moving clouds and, in the far distance, a hesitant sun casting rays on the volcanic black domes of the Pentland Hills.

He could restrict himself to thinking that Kirsten is rather a nice person with whom to spend a morning solving some vexing issues of municipal administration. He could curtail his judgement as to what depths of character could plausibly lie behind her reflections on office life and Scottish politics. He could accept that her soul is unlikely to be casually discernible in her pallor and the slope of her neck. He could be satisfied to say that she seems interesting enough and that he will need another twenty-five years to know much more.

Instead of which, Rabih feels certain that he has discovered someone endowed with the most extraordinary combination of inner and outer qualities – intelligence and kindness, humour and beauty, sincerity and courage; someone whom he would miss if she left the room even though she had been entirely unknown to him but two hours before; someone whose fingers – currently drawing faint lines with a toothpick across the tablecloth – he longs to caress and squeeze between his own; someone with whom he wants to spend the rest of his life.

Terrified of offending, unsure of her tastes, aware of the risk of misreading a cue, he shows her extreme solicitude and fine-grained attention.

'I'm sorry, would you prefer to hold your umbrella?' he asks as they make their way back to the site.

'Oh, I really don't mind,' she replies.

'I'd be happy to hold it for you – or not,' he presses.

'Really, whatever you want!'

He edits himself strictly. Whatever the pleasures of disclosure, he seeks to shield Kirsten from all but a few sides of his character. Showing his true self is not, at this stage, any kind of priority.

They meet again the following week. As they walk back towards the Taj Mahal for a budget and progress report, Rabih asks if he might give her a hand with the bag of files she is carrying, in response to which she laughs and tells him not to be so sexist. It doesn't seem the right moment to reveal that he would no less gladly help her to move house – or nurse her through malaria. Then again, it only amplifies Rabih's enthusiasm that Kirsten doesn't appear to need much help with anything all – weakness being, in the end, a charming prospect chiefly in the strong.

'The thing is half of my department has just been let go, so I'm effectively doing the work of three people,' Kirsten explains, once they are seated. 'I didn't finish till ten last night, though that's mostly because, as you may already have picked up, I am something of a control freak.'

So frightened is he of saying the wrong thing, he can't find anything to talk about – but because silence seems like proof of dullness, neither can he allow the pauses to go on. He ends up offering a lengthy description of how bridges distribute their loads across their piers, then follows up with an analysis of the relative braking speeds of tyres on wet and dry surfaces. His clumsiness is at least an incidental sign of his sincerity: we tend not to get very anxious when seducing people we don't much care about.

At every turn he senses the weakness of his claim upon Kirsten's attention. His impression of her freedom and autonomy scares as much as it excites him. He appreciates the lack of any good reasons why she would ever bestow her affections upon him. He properly understands how little right he has to ask her to look upon him with the kindness which his many limitations require. At the perimeter of Kirsten's life, he is at the apogee of modesty.

Then comes the pivotal challenge of knowing whether the feeling is mutual, a topic of almost childlike simplicity nonetheless capable of sustaining endless semiotic study and detailed psychological conjecture. She complimented him on his grey raincoat. She let him pay for their tea and poppadoms. She was encouraging when he mentioned his ambition to return to architecture. But then again, she seemed ill at ease, even a little irritated, on the three occasions when he tried to bring the conversation around to her past relationships. Nor did she pick up on his hint about catching a film.

Such doubts only inflame desire. As Rabih has realized, the most attractive people aren't those who accept him right away (he doubts their judgement) or those who never give him a chance (he grows to resent their indifference) but rather those who, for unfathomable reasons – perhaps a competing romantic entanglement or a cautious nature, a physical predicament or a psychological inhibition, a religious commitment or a political objection – leave him turning for a little while in the wind.

The longing proves, in its own way, exquisite.

Eventually, Rabih looks up her phone number in the council paperwork and, one Saturday morning, texts his opinion that it might be sunny later. 'I know,' comes the almost instantaneous reply. 'On for a trip to the Botanics? Kx'

Which is how they end up, three hours later, touring some of the world's most unusual tree and plant species in Edinburgh's Royal Botanic Garden. They see a Chilean orchid, they are struck by the complexity of a rhododendron and they pause between a fir tree from Switzerland and an immense redwood from Canada whose fronds stir in a light wind coming in off the sea.

Rabih has run out of energy to formulate the meaningless comments which typically precede such events. It is thus out of a sense of impatient despair rather than arrogance or entitlement that he cuts Kirsten off in mid-sentence as she reads from an information plaque – 'Alpine trees should never be confused with . . .' – takes her face in his hands and presses his lips gently against hers, to which she responds by shutting her eyes and wrapping her arms tightly around his lower back.

An ice cream van in Inverleith Terrace emits an eerie jingle, a jackdaw screeches on the branch of a tree transplanted from New Zealand and no one notices two people, partly hidden by non-native trees, in one of the more tender and consequential moments of both of their lives.

And yet, we should insist, none of this has anything much yet to do with a love story. Love stories begin not when we fear someone may be unwilling to see us again, but when they decide they would have no objection to seeing us all the time; not when they have every opportunity to run away, but when they have exchanged solemn vows promising to hold us, and be held captive by us, for life.

Our understanding of love has been hijacked and beguiled by its first distractingly moving moments. We have allowed our love stories to end way too early. We seem to know far too much about how love starts, and recklessly little about how it might continue.

At the gates to the Botanic Garden, Kirsten tells Rabih to call her and admits, with a smile in which he suddenly sees what she must have looked like when she was ten years old, that she'll be free any evening the following week.

On his walk home to Quartermile, wending through the Saturday crowds, Rabih is thrilled enough to want to stop random strangers and share his good fortune with them. He has, without knowing how, richly succeeded at the three central challenges underpinning the Romantic idea of love: he has found the right person, he has opened his heart to her and he has been accepted.

And yet he is, of course, nowhere yet. He and Kirsten will marry, they will suffer, they will frequently worry about money, they will have a girl first, then a boy, one of them will have an affair, there will be passages of boredom, they'll sometimes want to murder one another and on a few occasions to kill themselves. *This* will be the real love story.

In Love

Kirsten suggests a trip to Portobello Beach, half an hour away by bicycle on the Firth of Forth. Rabih is unsteady on his bike, rented from a shop that Kirsten knows off Princes Street. She has her own, a cherry-red model with twelve gears and advanced brake calipers. He does his best to keep up. Halfway down the hill, he activates a new gear but the chain protests, jumps and spins impotently against the hub. Frustration and a familiar rage surge up within him. It'll be a long walk back up to the shop. But this isn't Kirsten's way. 'Look at you,' she says, 'you big cross numpty, you.' She turns the bike upside down, reverses the gears and adjusts the rear derailleur. Her hands are soon smudged with oil, a streak of which ends up on her cheek.

Love means admiration for qualities in the lover that promise to correct our weaknesses and imbalances; love is a search for completion.

He has fallen in love with her calm, her faith that it will be OK, her lack of a sense of persecution, her absence of fatalism – these are the virtues of his unusual new Scottish friend who speaks in an accent so hard to understand that he has to ask three times for clarification on her use of the word *temporary*. Rabih's love is a logical response to the discovery of complementary strengths and a range of attributes to which he aspires. He loves from a feeling of incompleteness – and from a desire to be made whole.

He isn't alone in this. Albeit in different areas, Kirsten is likewise seeking to make up for deficiencies. She didn't travel outside Scotland until after university. Her relatives all come from the same small part of the country. Spirits are narrow there: the colours grey, the atmosphere provincial, the values self-denying. She is, in response, powerfully drawn to what she associates with the South. She wants light, hope, people who live through their bodies with passion and emotion. She reveres the sun while hating her own paleness and discomfort in its rays. There is a poster of the medina in Fez hanging on her wall.

She is excited by what she has learned about Rabih's background. She finds it intriguing that he is the son of a Lebanese civil-engineer father and a German air-hostess mother. He tells her stories about a childhood spent in Beirut, Athens and Barcelona, in which there were moments of brightness and beauty and, now and then, extreme danger. He speaks Arabic, French, German and Spanish; his endearments (playfully delivered) come in many flavours. His skin is olive to her rosy white. He crosses his long legs when he sits and his surprisingly delicate hands know how to prepare her *makdous*, *tabbouleh* and *Kartoffelsalat*. He feeds her his worlds.

She, too, is looking for love to rebalance and complete her.

Love is also, and equally, about weakness, about being touched by another's fragilities and sorrows, especially when (as happens in the early days) we ourselves are in no danger of being held responsible for them. Seeing our lover despondent and in crisis, in tears and unable to cope, can reassure us that, for all their virtues, they are not alienatingly invincible. They, too, are at points confused and at sea, a realization which lends us a new supportive role, reduces our sense of shame about our own inadequacies and draws us closer to each other around a shared experience of pain.

They take the train to Inverness to visit Kirsten's mother. She insists on coming to meet them at the station, though it means a bus journey from the opposite side of town. She calls Kirsten her 'Lambie' and hugs her tightly on the platform, her eyes closed achingly. She extends a hand formally to Rabih and apologizes for the conditions at this time of year: it is two thirty in the afternoon and already nearly dark. She has the same vivacious eyes as her daughter, though hers have an additional, unflinching quality that causes him to feel rather uncomfortable when they settle on him – as they are to do repeatedly, and without apparent occasion, during their stay.

Home is a narrow, two-storey, grey terraced house located directly opposite the primary school where Kirsten's mother has been teaching for three decades. All around Inverness there are grown-ups – now running shops, drafting contracts and drawing blood samples – who can remember their introduction to basic arithmetic and the Bible stories at Mrs McLelland's knee. More specifically, most recall her distinctive way of letting them know not only how much she liked them but also how easily they might disappoint her.

The three of them eat supper together in the living room while watching a quiz show on TV. Drawings that Kirsten made in nursery school march up the wall along the staircase in neat gilt frames. In the hall there is a photograph of her baptism; in the kitchen, a portrait of her in her school uniform, sensible-looking and gap-toothed at age seven; and on the bookshelf, a snapshot from when she was eleven, bone-thin, tousled and intrepid in shorts and a T-shirt at the beach.

In her bedroom, more or less untouched since she went to Aberdeen to take a degree in law and accountancy, there are black clothes in the wardrobe and shelves packed with creased school paperbacks. Inside the Penguin edition of *Mansfield Park*, an adolescent version of Kirsten has written, 'Fanny Price: the virtue of the exceptional ordinary'. A photo album under the bed offers up a candid shot of her with her father, standing in front of an ice cream van at Cruden Bay. She is six and will have him in her life for one more year.

Family folklore has it that Kirsten's father upped and left one morning, having packed a small suitcase while his wife of ten years was off teaching. The sole explanation he provided was a slip of paper on the hallway table with *Sorry* scrawled on it. Thereafter he drifted around Scotland, taking up odd jobs on farms, keeping in touch with Kirsten only through an annual card and a gift on her birthday. When she turned twelve, a package arrived containing a cardigan fit for a nine-year-old. Kirsten sent it back to an address in Cammachmore, along with a note advising the sender of her frank hope that he would die soon. There has been no word from him since.

Had he left for another woman, he would merely have betrayed his wedding vows. But to leave his wife and child simply to be by himself, to have more of his own company, without ever furnishing a satisfactory account of his motives – this was rejection of an altogether deeper, more abstract and more devastating nature.

Kirsten lies in Rabih's arms while explaining. Her eyes are red. This is another part of her he loves: the weakness of the deeply able and competent person.

On her side, she feels much the same about him – and in his own history there are no less sorrowful circumstances to recount. When Rabih was twelve, after a childhood marked by sectarian violence, roadblocks and nights spent in air-raid shelters, he and his parents quit Beirut for Barcelona. But only half a year after they had arrived there and settled into a flat near the old docks, his mother began to complain of a pain near her abdomen. She went to the doctor and, with an unexpectedness that would deal an irremediable blow to her son's faith in the solidity of pretty much anything, received a diagnosis of advanced liver cancer. She was dead three months later. Within a year his father was remarried, to an emotionally distant Englishwoman with whom he now lives in retirement in an apartment in Cádiz.

Kirsten wants, with an intensity that surprises her, to comfort the twelve-year-old boy across the decades. Her mind keeps returning to a picture of Rabih and his mother, taken two years before her death, on the tarmac at Beirut Airport, with a Lufthansa jet behind them. Rabih's mother worked on flights to Asia and America, serving meals at the front of the aircraft to wealthy businessmen, making sure seat belts were fastened, pouring drinks and smiling at strangers, while her son waited for her at home. Rabih remembers the overexcited near-nausea he felt on the days she was due to return. From Japan she once brought him some notebooks made of fibre from mulberry trees, and from Mexico a painted figurine of an Aztec chief. She looked like a film actress – Romy Schneider, people said.

At the centre of Kirsten's love is a desire to heal the wound of Rabih's long-buried, largely unmentioned loss.

Love reaches a pitch at those moments when our beloved turns out to understand, more clearly than others have ever been able to, and perhaps even better than we do ourselves, the chaotic, embarrassing and shameful

*parts of us. That someone else gets who we are and both sympathizes
with and forgives us for what they see underpins our whole capacity to
trust and to give. Love is a dividend of gratitude for our lover's insight
into our own confused and troubled psyche.*

'You're in your "angry-and-humiliated-yet-strangely-quiet" mode
again,' she diagnoses one evening when the car rental website
Rabih has used to book himself and four colleagues a minibus
freezes on him at the very last screen, leaving in doubt whether it
has properly understood his intentions and debited his card. 'I think
you should scream, say something rude, then come to bed. I
wouldn't mind. I might even call the rental place for you in the
morning.' She somehow sees right into his inability to express his
anger; she recognizes the process whereby he converts difficulty
into numbness and self-disgust. Without shaming him, she can
identify and name the forms his madness sometimes takes.

With similar accuracy, she grasps his fear of seeming unworthy
in his father's eyes and, by extension, in the eyes of other male
figures of authority. On their way into a first meeting with his
father at the George Hotel, she whispers to Rabih without preamble, 'Just imagine if it didn't matter what he thought of me – or,
come to think of it, of you.' To Rabih, it feels as if he were returning
with a friend in broad daylight to a forest he'd only ever been in
alone and at night and could see that the malevolent figures which
had once terrified him were really, all along, just boulders that had
caught the shadows at the wrong angles.

*There is, in the early period of love, a measure of sheer relief at being
able, at last, to reveal so much of what needed to be kept hidden for the
sake of propriety. We can admit to not being as respectable or as sober,
as even-keeled or as 'normal', as society believes. We can be childish,*

imaginative, wild, hopeful, cynical, fragile and multiple — all of this our lover can understand and accept us for.

At eleven at night, with one supper already behind them, they go out for another, fetching barbecued ribs from Los Argentinos, in Preston Street, which they then eat by moonlight on a bench in the Meadows. They speak to each other in funny accents: she is a lost tourist from Hamburg looking for the Museum of Modern Art; he can't be of much help because, as a lobsterman from Aberdeen, he can't understand her unusual intonation.

They are back in the playful spirit of childhood. They bounce on the bed. They swap piggyback rides. They gossip. After attending a party, they inevitably end up finding fault with all the other guests, their loyalty to each other deepened by their ever-increasing disloyalty towards everyone else.

They are in revolt against the hypocrisies of their usual lives. They free each other from compromise. They share a sense of having no more secrets.

They must normally answer to names imposed on them by the rest of the world, used on official documents and by government bureaucracies, but love inspires them to cast around for nicknames that will more precisely accord with the respective sources of their tenderness. Kirsten thus becomes 'Teckle', the Scottish colloquialism for 'great', which to Rabih sounds impish and ingenuous, nimble and determined. He, meanwhile, becomes 'Sfouf', after the dry Lebanese cake flavoured with aniseed and turmeric that he introduces her to in a delicatessen in Nicolson Square – and which perfectly captures for her the reserved sweetness and Levantine exoticism of the sad-eyed boy from Beirut.

Sex and Love

For their second date, after the kiss in the Botanic Garden, Rabih has suggested dinner at a Thai restaurant on Howe Street. He arrives there first and is shown to a table in the basement, next to an aquarium alarmingly crowded with lobsters. She's a few minutes late, dressed very casually in an old pair of jeans and trainers, wearing no make-up and glasses rather than her usual contact lenses. The conversation starts off awkwardly. To Rabih there seems no way to reconnect with the greater intimacy of the last time they were together. It's as if they were back to being only acquaintances again. They talk about his mother and her father and some books and films they both know. But he doesn't dare to touch her hands, which she keeps mostly in her lap anyway. It seems natural to imagine she may have changed her mind.

Yet once they're out in the street afterwards, the tension dissipates. 'Do you fancy a tea at mine – something herbal?' she asks. 'It's not far from here.'

So they walk a few streets over to a block of flats and climb up to the top floor, where she has a tiny yet beautiful one-bedroom place with views on to the sea and, along the walls, photographs she has taken of different parts of the Highlands. Rabih gets a glimpse of the bedroom, where there's a huge pile of clothes in a mess on the bed.

'I tried on pretty much everything I own and then I thought, To hell with that,' she calls out, 'as one does!'

She's in the kitchen, brewing tea. He wanders in, picks up the box and remarks how odd the word *chamomile* looks written down. 'You notice all the most important things,' she jokes warmly. It feels like an invitation of sorts, so he moves towards her and gently kisses her. The kiss goes on for a long time. In the background they hear the kettle boil, then subside. Rabih wonders how much further he might go. He strokes the back of Kirsten's neck, then her shoulders. He braves a tentative caress over her chest and waits in vain for a reaction. His right hand makes a foray over her jeans, very lightly, and traces a line down both her thighs. He knows he may now be at the outer limits of what would be fitting on a second date. Still, he risks venturing down with his hand once again, this time moving a bit more purposefully against the jeans, pressing in rhythm between her legs.

That begins one of the most erotic moments of Rabih's life, for when Kirsten feels his hand pressing against her through her jeans, she thrusts forward ever so slightly to greet it, and then a bit more. She opens her eyes and smiles at him, as he does back at her.

'Just there,' she says, focusing his hand on one very specific area to the side of the lower part of her zip.

This goes on for another minute or so, and then she reaches down and takes his wrist, moves the hand up a little and guides him to undo her button. Together they open her jeans, and she takes his hand and invites it inside the black elastic of her pants. He feels her warmth and, a second later, a wetness that symbolizes an unambiguous welcome and excitement.

Sexiness might at first appear to be a merely physiological phenomenon, the result of awakened hormones and stimulated nerve endings. But in truth it is not so much about sensations as it is about ideas — foremost among them, the idea of acceptance, and the promise of an end to loneliness and shame.

Her jeans are wide open now, and both of their faces are flushed. From Rabih's perspective, the sexiness, which is a blend of relief and excitement, springs in part from the fact that Kirsten gave so little indication over so long that she really had such things on her mind.

She leads him into the bedroom and kicks the pile of clothes on to the floor. On the bedside table is the novel she's been reading by George Sand, whom Rabih has never heard of. There are some earrings, too, and a picture of Kirsten in a uniform standing outside her primary school, holding her mother's hand.

'I didn't have a chance to hide all my secrets,' she says. 'But don't let that hold you back from snooping.'

There's an almost full moon out and they leave the curtains open. As they lie entwined on the bed, he strokes her hair and squeezes her hand. Their smiles suggest they're not completely past shyness yet. He pauses in mid-caress and asks when she first decided she might want this, prompted in his enquiry not by vanity but by a mixture of gratitude and liberation, now that desires which might have seemed simply obscene, predatory or pitiful in their unanswered form have proved to be redemptively mutual.

'Pretty early on, actually, Mr Khan,' she says. 'Is there anything more I can help you with?'

'As a matter of fact, yes.'

'Go on.'

'OK, so at what point did you first feel, you know, that you might . . . how can I say . . . well, that you'd perhaps be on for . . .'

'Fucking you?'

'Something like that.'

'Now I see what you mean,' she teases. 'To tell you the truth, it started that very first time we walked over to the restaurant. I noticed you had a nice bum, and I kept thinking about it all the while you were boring on about the work we had to do – and then later that night I was imagining, stretched out on this very bed that we're on right now, what it would be like to get hold of your . . . Well, OK, I'm going to get shy now, too, so that may have to be it for the moment.'

That respectable-looking people might be inwardly harbouring some beautifully carnal and explicit fantasies, while outwardly seeming to care only about friendly banter – this still strikes Rabih as somehow an entirely surprising and deeply delightful concept, with the immediate power to soothe a raft of his own underlying guilty feelings about his sexuality. That Kirsten's late-night fantasies might have been about him, when she had seemed so reserved at the time, and that she was now so eager and so direct – these revelations mark out the moment as among the very best of Rabih's life.

For all the talk of sexual liberation, the truth is that secrecy and a degree of embarrassment around sex continue as much as they have always done. We still can't generally say what we want to do and with whom. Shame and repression of impulse aren't just things that our ancestors and certain buttoned-up religions latched on to for obscure and unnecessary reasons: they are fated to be constants in all eras – which is what lends such power to those rare moments (there might be only a few in a lifetime) when a stranger invites us to drop our guard and admits to wanting pretty much exactly what we had once privately and guiltily craved.

It is two in the morning by the time they finish. An owl is hooting somewhere in the darkness.

Kirsten falls asleep in Rabih's arms. She seems trustful and at ease, slipping gracefully into the current of sleep while he stands at the shore, protesting against the end of this miraculous day, rehearsing its pivotal moments. He watches her lips tremble slightly, as though she were reading a book to herself in some foreign language of the night. Occasionally she seems to wake for an instant and, looking startled and scared, appeals for help: 'The train!' she exclaims, or, with even greater alarm, 'It's tomorrow, they moved it!' He reassures her (they have enough time to get to the station; she's done all the necessary revision for the exam) and takes her hand, like a parent preparing to lead a child across a busy road.

It's more than mere coyness to refer to what they have done as 'making love'. They haven't just had sex; they have translated their feelings – appreciation, tenderness, gratitude and surrender – into a physical act.

We call things a turn-on but what we might really be alluding to is delight at finally having been allowed to reveal our secret selves – and at discovering that, far from being horrified by who we are, our lovers have opted to respond with only encouragement and approval.

A degree of shame and a habit of secrecy surrounding sex began for Rabih when he was twelve. Before that there were, of course, a few minor lies told and transgressions committed: he stole some coins from his father's wallet; he merely pretended to like his aunt Ottilie, and one afternoon in her stuffy, cramped apartment by the Corniche, he copied a whole section of his algebra homework from his brilliant classmate Michel. But none of those infractions caused him to feel any primal self-disgust.

For his mother, he had always been the sweet, thoughtful child she called by the diminutive nickname 'Maus'. Maus liked to cuddle with her under the large cashmere blanket in the living room and to have his hair stroked away from his smooth forehead. Then one term, all of a sudden, the only thing Maus could think about was a group of girls a couple of years above him at school, five or six feet tall, articulate Spaniards who walked around at break-time in a conspiratorial gang and giggled together with a cruel, confident and enticing air. At weekends he would slip into the little blue bathroom at home every few hours and visualize scenes that he'd will himself to forget again the moment he was finished. A chasm opened up between who he had to be for his family and who he knew he was inside. The disjuncture was perhaps most painful in relation to his mother. It didn't help that the onset of puberty coincided for him almost exactly with the diagnosis of her cancer. Deep in his unconscious, in some dark recess immune to logic, he nursed the impression that his discovery of sex might have helped to kill her.

Things weren't completely straightforward for Kirsten at that age, either. For her, too, there were oppressive ideas at play about what it meant to be a good person. At fourteen she liked walking the dog, volunteering at the old people's home, doing extra geography homework about rivers – but also, alone in her bedroom, lying on the floor with her skirt hiked up, watching herself in the mirror and imagining that she was putting on a show for an older boy at school. Much like Rabih, she wanted certain things which didn't seem to fit in with the dominant, socially prescribed notions of normality.

These past histories of self-division are part of what makes the beginning of their relationship so satisfying. There is no more need for subterfuge or furtiveness between them. Although they have both had a number of partners in the past, they find each other exceptionally open-minded and reassuring. Kirsten's bedroom becomes the headquarters for nightly explorations during which they are at last able to disclose, without fear of being judged, the many unusual and improbable things that their sexuality compels them to crave.

The particulars of what arouses us may sound odd and illogical, but seen from close up they carry echoes of qualities we long for in other, purportedly saner areas of existence: understanding, sympathy, trust, unity, generosity and kindness. Beneath many erotic triggers lie symbolic solutions to some of our greatest fears, and poignant allusions to our yearnings for friendship and understanding.

It's three weeks now since their first time. Rabih runs his fingers roughly through Kirsten's hair. She indicates, by a movement of her head and a little sigh, that she would like rather more of that – and harder, too, please. She wants her lover to bunch her hair in his hand and pull it with some violence. For Rabih it's a tricky development. He has been taught to treat women with great respect, to hold the two genders as equal and to believe that neither person in a relationship should ever wield power over the other. But right now his partner appears to have scant interest in equality, nor much concern for the ordinary rules of gender balance, either.

She's no less keen on a range of problematic words. She invites him to address her as though he cared nothing for her, and they both find this exciting precisely because the very opposite is true. The epithets *bastard*, *bitch* and *cunt* become shared tokens of their mutual loyalty and trust.

In bed, violence – normally such a danger – no longer has to be a risk; a degree of force can be expended safely and won't make either of them unhappy. Rabih's momentary fury can remain entirely within his control even as Kirsten draws from it an empowering sense of her own resilience.

As children they were both often physical with their friends. It could be fun to hit. Kirsten would whack her cousins hard with the sofa pillows, while Rabih would wrestle with his friends on the grass at the swimming club. In adulthood, however, violence of any kind has been prohibited; no grown person is ever supposed to use force against another. And yet within the boundaries of the couple's games, it can feel strangely pleasing to take a swipe, to hit a little and be hit; they can be rough and insistent; there can be a savage edge. Within the protective circle of their love, neither of them has to feel in any danger of being hurt or left bereft.

Kirsten is a woman of considerable steeliness and authority. She manages a department at work, she earns more than her lover, she is confident and a leader. She has known from a young age that she must be able to take care of herself.

However, in bed with Rabih, she now discovers that she'd like to assume a different role, as a form of escape from the wearying demands of the rest of her life. Her being submissive to him means allowing a loving person to tell her exactly what to do, letting him take responsibility and choice away from her.

The idea has never appealed to her before, but only because she believed that most bossy people were not to be trusted: they didn't seem, as Rabih does, truly kind and utterly non-violent by nature (she playfully calls him Sultan Khan). She's craved independence in part by default, because there have been no Ottoman potentates around who were nice enough to deserve her weaker self.

For his part, Rabih has all his adult life had to keep his bossiness sharply in check, and yet in his deeper self, he's aware of having a sterner side to his nature. He is sometimes sure he knows what's best for other people and what they rightly have coming to them. In the real world he may be a powerless minor associate in a provincial urban design firm, with strong inhibitions around expressing what he really thinks, but in bed with Kirsten he can feel the appeal of casting aside his customary reserve and enforcing absolute obedience, just as Suleiman the Magnificent might have done in his harem in the marble and jade palace on the shores of the Bosphorus.

The games of submission and domination, the rule-breaking scenarios, the fetishistic interest in particular words or parts of the body: all offer opportunities to investigate wishes that are far from being simply peculiar, pointless or slightly demented. They offer brief utopian interludes in which we can, with a rare and real friend, safely cast off our normal defences and share and satisfy our longings for extreme closeness and mutual acceptance – which is the real, psychologically rooted reason why games are, in the end, so exciting.

They fly to Amsterdam for a weekend and midway there, over the North Sea, elope to the toilet. They've discovered an enthusiasm for having a go at it in semi-public places, which seems to bring into sudden, risky but electrifying alignment both their sexual sides and the more formal public personae they normally have to present. They feel as though they are challenging responsibility, anonymity and restraint with their uninhibited and heated moments. Their pleasure becomes somehow the more intense for the presence of 240 oblivious passengers only one thin door panel away.

It's cramped in the bathroom, but Kirsten manages to unzip Rabih and take him into her mouth. She has mostly resisted doing this with other men in the past, but with him the act has become a constant and compelling extension of her love. To receive the apparently dirtiest, most private, guiltiest part of her lover into the most public, most respectable part of herself is symbolically to free them both from the punishing dichotomy between dirty and clean, bad and good – in the process, as they fly through the glacial lower atmosphere towards Scheveningen at 400 kilometres an hour, making whole their previously divided and shamed selves.

The Proposal

Over Christmas, their first spent together, they return to Kirsten's mother's house in Inverness. Mrs McLelland shows him maternal kindness (new socks, a book on Scottish birds, a hot-water bottle for his single bed) and, though it is skilfully concealed, constant curiosity. Her enquiries, beside the kitchen sink after a meal or on a walk around the ruins of St Andrew's Cathedral, have a surface casualness to them, but Rabih is under no illusion. He is being interviewed. She wants to understand his family, his previous relationships, how his work in London came to an end and what his responsibilities are in Edinburgh. He is being assessed as much as he can be in an age which doesn't allow for parental vetting and which insists that relationships will work best if no outside arbiters are awarded authority — for romantic unions should be the unique prerogative of the individuals concerned, excluding even those who may have — not so many years ago — given one of the pair her bath every evening and, at weekends, taken her to Bught Park in a pram to throw bread to the pigeons.

Having no say does not mean, however, that Mrs McLelland has no questions. She wonders if Rabih will prove to be a philanderer or a spendthrift, a weakling or a drunk, a bore or the sort to resolve an argument with a little force — and she is curious because she knows, better than most, that there is no one more likely to destroy us than the person we marry.

When, on their last day together, Mrs McLelland remarks to Rabih over lunch what a pity it is that Kirsten never sang another note after her father left home, because she had a particularly promising voice and a place in the treble section of the choir, she isn't just sharing a detail of her daughter's former extracurricular activities; she is — as much as the rules allow — asking Rabih not to ruin Kirsten's life.

They take the train back to Edinburgh the evening before New Year's Eve, a four-hour ride across the Highlands in harness to an ageing diesel. Kirsten, a veteran of the journey, has known to bring along a blanket, in which they wrap themselves in the empty rear carriage. Seen from distant farms, the train must look like an illuminated line, no larger than a millipede, making its way across a pane of blackness.

Kirsten seems preoccupied.

'No, nothing at all,' she replies when he asks, but no sooner has she uttered her denial than a tear wells up, more rapidly followed by a second and a third. Still, it really is nothing, she stresses. She is being silly. A dunderhead. She doesn't mean to embarrass him, all men hate this kind of thing, and she doesn't plan to make it a habit. Most importantly, it has nothing to do with him. It is her mother. She is crying because, for the first time in her adult life, she feels properly happy — a happiness which her own mother, with whom she has an almost symbiotic connection, has so seldom known. Mrs McLelland worries that Rabih might make her sad; Kirsten cries with guilt at how happy her lover has helped her to become.

He holds her close to him. They don't speak. They have known each other for a little over six months. It wasn't his plan to bring this up now. But just past the village of Killiecrankie, after the ticket collector's visit, Rabih turns to face Kirsten and asks, without preamble, if she will marry him, not necessarily right away, he adds, but whenever she feels it is right, and not necessarily with any fuss, either, it could be a tiny occasion, just them and her mother and a few friends, but of course it could be bigger too if that's what she prefers; the key thing is that he loves her without reservation and wants, more than anything he's ever wanted before, to be with her as long as he lives.

She turns away and is, for a short while, perfectly silent. She isn't very good at these sorts of moments, she confesses, not that they often happen, or indeed ever. She doesn't have a speech ready, this has come like a bolt from the blue, but how different it is from what ordinarily happens to her, how deeply kind and mad and courageous of him to come out with something like this now – and yet, despite her cynical character and her firm belief that she doesn't care for these things, so long as he has truly understood what he wants and has noted what a monster she is, then she can't really see why she wouldn't say, with all her heart and with immense fear and gratitude, yes, yes, yes.

It tells us something about the relative status of rigorous analysis in the nuptial process that it would be considered un-Romantic, and even mean, to ask an engaged couple to explain in any depth, with patience and self-awareness, what exactly had led them to make and accept a proposal. And yet we're keen, of course, always to ask where and how the proposal took place.

It isn't disrespectful to Rabih to suggest that he doesn't really know why he has asked her to marry him, *know* in the sense of being in command of a rationally founded, coherent set of motives which could be shared with a sceptical or probing third party. What he has instead of a rationale is feelings, and plenty of them: the feeling of never wanting to let her go because of her broad open forehead and the way her upper lip protrudes ever so slightly over her lower one; the feeling that he loves her because of her furtive, slightly surprised quick-witted air which inspires him to call her his 'Rat' and his 'Mole' (and which also, because her looks are unconventional, makes him feel clever for finding her attractive); the feeling that he needs to marry her because of the diligent concentration on her face when she prepares a cod and spinach pie, because of her sweetness when she buttons up her duffel coat and because of the cunning intelligence she displays when she unpacks the psyches of people they know.

There is virtually no serious thought underpinning his certainty about marriage. He has never read any books on the institution, he has in the last decade never spent more than ten minutes with a baby, he has never cynically interrogated a married couple let alone spoken in any depth with a divorced one and would be at a loss to explain why the majority of marriages fail, save from the general idiocy or lack of imagination of their participants.

For most of recorded history, people married for logical sorts of reasons: because her parcel of land adjoined his, his family had a flourishing grain business, her father was the magistrate in town, there was a castle to keep up, or both sets of parents subscribed to the same interpretation of a holy text. And from such reasonable marriages, there flowed loneliness, rape, infidelity, beating, hardness of heart and screams heard through the nursery doors.

The marriage of reason was not, from any sincere perspective, reasonable at all; it was often expedient, narrow-minded, snobbish, exploitative and abusive. Which is why what has replaced it — the marriage of feeling — has largely been spared the need to account for itself. What matters is that two people wish desperately for it to happen, are drawn to one another by an overwhelming instinct and know in their hearts that it is right. The modern age appears to have had enough of 'reasons', those catalysts of misery, those accountants' demands. Indeed the more imprudent a marriage appears (perhaps it's been only six weeks since they met; one of them has no job or both are barely out of their teens), the safer it may actually be deemed to be, for apparent 'recklessness' is taken as a counterweight to all the errors and tragedies vouchsafed by the so-called sensible unions of old. The prestige of instinct is the legacy of a collective traumatized reaction against too many centuries of unreasonable 'reason'.

He asks her to marry him because it feels like an extremely danger-ous thing to do: if the marriage were to fail, it would ruin both their lives. Those voices which hint that marriage is no longer necessary, that it is far safer simply to cohabit, are right from a practical point of view, concedes Rabih, but they miss the emo-tional appeal of danger, of putting oneself and one's beloved through an experience that could, with only a few twists of the plotline, result in mutual destruction. Rabih takes his very willing-ness to be ruined in love's name as proof of his commitment. That it is 'unnecessary' in the practical sense to marry serves only to render the idea more compelling emotionally. *Being* married may be associated with caution, conservatism and timidity, but *getting* married is an altogether different, more reckless and therefore more appealingly Romantic proposition.

Marriage, to Rabih, feels like the high point of a daring path to total intimacy; proposing has all the passionate allure of shutting one's eyes and jumping off a steep cliff, wishing and trusting that the other will be there to catch one.

He proposes because he wants to preserve, to 'freeze', what he and Kirsten feel for each other. He hopes through the act of marrying to make an ecstatic sensation perpetual.

There is one memory he'll return to again and again in recalling the fervour he wants to hold on to. They are at a rooftop club on George Street. It is a Saturday night. They are on the dance floor, bathed in rapid orbits of purple and yellow lights, with a hip-hop bass alternating with the rousing choruses of stadium anthems. She's wearing trainers, black velvet shorts and a black chiffon top. He wants to lick the sweat off her temples and swing her around in his arms. The music and the fellowship among the dancers promise a permanent end to all pain and division.

They go out on to a terrace illuminated only by a series of large candles distributed around the railings. It's a clear night and the universe has come down to meet them. She points out Andromeda. A plane banks over Edinburgh Castle, then straightens up for the descent to the airport. In the moment he feels beyond doubt that this is the woman he wants to grow old with.

There are, of course, quite a few aspects of this occasion which marriage could not enable him to 'freeze' or preserve: the serenity of the vast, star-filled night; the generous hedonism of the Dionysian club; the absence of responsibility; the indolent Sunday that lies before them (they will sleep until midday); her buoyant mood and his sense of gratitude. Rabih is not marrying – and therefore fixing for ever – a feeling. He is marrying a person with whom, under a very particular, privileged and fugitive set of circumstances, he has been fortunate enough to share a feeling.

The proposal is at one level about what he's running towards but also, and perhaps every bit as much, about what he's running away from. A few months before he met Kirsten, he had dinner with a couple – old friends from his days at university in Salamanca.

They had a lively meal, catching up on news. As the three of them were leaving the restaurant in Victoria Street, Marta smoothed down the collar of Juan's camel-coloured coat and wrapped his burgundy scarf carefully around his neck, a gesture of such natural and tender care that it had the incidental effect of making Rabih appreciate – like a punch in the stomach – how entirely alone he was in a world wholly indifferent to his existence and fate.

Life on his own had become, he realized then, untenable. He had had enough of solitary walks home at the end of desultory parties, of entire Sundays passed without speaking a word to another human, of holidays spent tagging along with harassed couples whose children left them no energy for conversation, of the knowledge that he occupied no important place in anyone's heart.

He loves Kirsten deeply, but he hates the idea of being on his own with almost equal force.

To a shameful extent, the charm of marriage boils down to how unpleasant it is to be alone. This isn't necessarily our fault as individuals. Society as a whole appears determined to render the single state as nettlesome and depressing as possible: once the freewheeling days of school and university are over, company and warmth become dispiritingly hard to find; social life starts to revolve oppressively around couples; there's no one left to call or hang out with. It's hardly surprising, then, if when we find someone halfway decent, we might cling.

In the old days, when people could (in theory) only have sex after they were married, wise observers knew that some might be tempted to marry for the wrong reasons – and so argued that the taboos around premarital sex should be lifted to help the young make calmer, less impulse-driven choices.

But if that particular impediment to good judgement has been removed, another kind of hunger seems to have taken its place. The longing for company may be no less powerful or irresponsible in its effects than the sexual motive once was. Spending fifty-two straight Sundays alone may play havoc with a person's prudence. Loneliness can provoke an unhelpful rush and repression of doubt and ambivalence about a potential spouse. The success of any relationship should be determined not just by how happy a couple are to be together, but by how worried each partner would be about not being in a relationship at all.

He proposes with such confidence and certainty because he believes himself to be a really rather straightforward person to live alongside – another tricky circumstantial result of having been on his own for a very long time. The single state has a habit of promoting a mistaken self-image of normalcy. Rabih's tendency to tidy obsessively when he feels chaotic inside, his habit of using work to ward off his anxieties, the difficulty he has in articulating what's on his mind when he's worried, his fury when he can't find a favourite T-shirt – these eccentricities are all neatly obscured so long as there is no one else around to see him, let alone to create a mess, request that he come and eat his dinner, comment sceptically on his habit of cleaning the TV remote control or ask him to explain what he's fretting about. Without witnesses, he can operate under the benign illusion that he may just, with the right person, prove no particular challenge to be around.

A few centuries from now, the level of self-knowledge that our own age judges necessary to get married might be thought puzzling, if not outright barbaric. By then, a standard, wholly non-judgemental line of enquiry (appropriate even on a first date), to which everyone would be expected to have a tolerant, good-natured and non-defensive answer, would simply be: 'So in what ways are you mad?'

Kirsten tells Rabih that as a teenager she was unhappy, felt unable to connect with others and went through a phase of self-harming. Scratching her arms until they bled, she says, gave her the only relief she could find. Rabih feels moved by her admission, but it goes further than that: he is positively drawn to Kirsten because of her troubles. He identifies her as a suitable candidate for marriage because he is instinctively suspicious of people for whom things have always gone well. Around cheerful and sociable others he feels isolated and peculiar. He dislikes carefree types with a vengeance. In the past he has described certain women he has been out on dates with as 'boring', when anyone else might more generously and accurately have labelled them 'healthy'. Taking trauma to be a primary route to growth and depth, Rabih wants his own sadness to find an echo in his partner's character. He therefore doesn't much mind, initially, that Kirsten is sometimes withdrawn and hard to read, or that she tends to seem aloof and defensive in the extreme after they've had an argument. He entertains a confused wish to help her, without, however, understanding that help can be a challenging gift to deliver to those who are most in need of it. He interprets her damaged aspects in the most obvious and most lyrical way: as a chance for him to play a useful role.

We believe we are seeking happiness in love, but what we are really after is familiarity. We are looking to re-create, within our adult relationships, the very feelings we knew so well in childhood – and which were rarely limited to just tenderness and care. The love most of us will have tasted early on came entwined with other, more destructive dynamics: feelings of wanting to help an adult who was out of control, of being deprived of a parent's warmth or scared of his or her anger, or of not feeling secure enough to communicate our trickier wishes.

How logical, then, that we should as adults find ourselves rejecting

certain candidates not because they are wrong but because they are a
little too right — *in the sense of seeming somehow excessively balanced,*
mature, understanding and reliable — given that, in our hearts, such
rightness feels foreign and unearned. We chase after more exciting
others, not in the belief that life with them will be more harmonious,
but out of an unconscious sense that it will be reassuringly familiar in
its patterns of frustration.

He asks her to marry him in order to break the all-consuming grip
that the thought of relationships has for too long had on his psyche.
He is exhausted by seventeen years' worth of melodrama and
excitements that have led nowhere. He is thirty-two and restless
for other challenges. It's neither cynical nor callous of Rabih to feel
immense love for Kirsten and yet at the same time to hope that
marriage may conclusively end love's mostly painful dominion
over his life.

As for Kirsten, suffice to say (for we will be travelling mostly
in his mind) that we shouldn't underestimate the appeal to someone
who has often and painfully doubted many things, not least herself,
of a proposal from an ostensibly kind and interesting person who
seems unequivocally and emphatically convinced that she is right
for him.

They are married by an official in a salmon-pink room at the
Inverness register office on a rainy morning in November, in the
presence of her mother, his father and stepmother and eight of their
friends. They read out a set of vows supplied by the government
of Scotland, promising that they will love and care for each other,
that they will be patient and show compassion, that they will trust
and forgive and that they will remain best friends and loyal companions until death.

Uninclined to sound didactic (or perhaps simply unsure how to be so), the government offers no further suggestions about ways to concretize these vows – though it does present the couple with some information on the tax discounts available to those adding insulation to their first homes.

After the ceremony, the members of the wedding party repair to a nearby restaurant for lunch, and by late that same evening the new husband and wife are ensconced in a small hotel near Saint-Germain, in Paris.

Marriage: a hopeful, generous, infinitely kind gamble taken by two people who don't know yet who they are or who the other might be, binding themselves to a future they cannot conceive of and have carefully omitted to investigate.

EVER AFTER

Silly Things

In the City of Love, the Scottish wife and her Middle Eastern husband visit the dead at the cemetery of Père Lachaise. They search in vain for the bones of Jean de Brunhoff and end up sharing a croque monsieur on top of Edith Piaf. Back in their room, they pull off what Kirsten calls the 'spermy bedcover', spread a towel out and, on paper plates and with the help of plastic forks, eat a dressed lobster from Brittany which called to them from the window of a deli in the rue du Cherche-Midi.

Opposite their hotel, a chichi children's boutique sells overpriced cardigans and dungarees. While Rabih is soaking in the bath one afternoon, Kirsten pops in and returns with Dobbie, a small furry monster with one horn and three deliberately ill-matched eyes, who, in six years' time, will become their daughter's favourite possession.

On their return to Scotland, they start to look for a flat. Rabih has married a rich woman, he jokes, which is true only in comparison with his own financial status. She owns a little place already, has been working for four years longer than he has and wasn't unemployed for eight months along the way. He has money enough to pay for the equivalent of a broom cupboard, she remarks (kindly). They find somewhere they like on the first floor of a building on

Merchiston Avenue. The seller is a frail, elderly widow who lost
her husband a year ago and whose two sons now live in Canada.
She isn't so well herself. Photos of the family when the boys were
young line a bank of dark-brown shelves which Rabih promptly
begins sizing up for a TV. He'll strip off the wallpaper, too, and
repaint the vivid orange kitchen cabinets in a more dignified
colour.

'You two remind me a little of how Ernie and I were in our day,'
says the old lady, and Kirsten answers, 'Bless,' and briefly puts an
arm around her. The seller used to be a magistrate; she now has an
inoperable tumour growing inside her spine and is moving to
sheltered accommodation on the other side of town. They settle
on a decent price; the seller isn't pushing the young couple as hard
as she might do. On the day they sign the contract, while Kirsten
ventures into the bedroom to take measurements, the old lady holds
Rabih back for an instant with a remarkably strong yet bony
hand. 'Be kind to her, won't you,' she says, 'even if you sometimes
think she's in the wrong.' Half a year later, they learn the seller
passed away.

They've reached the point where, by rights, their story – always
slight – should draw to a close. The Romantic challenge is behind
them. Life will from now on assume a steady, repetitive rhythm,
to the extent that they will often find it hard to locate a specific
event in time, so similar will the years appear in their outward
form. But their story is far from over: it is just a question of hence-
forth having to stand for longer in the stream and use a
smaller-meshed sieve to catch the grains of interest.

One Saturday morning, a few weeks after moving into the new
flat, Rabih and Kirsten drive to the big IKEA on the outskirts of
town to buy some glasses. The selection stretches over two aisles
and a multitude of styles. The previous weekend, in a new shop off

Queen Street, they swiftly found a lamp they both loved, with a wooden base and a porcelain shade. This should be easy.

Not long after entering the cavernous homeware department, Kirsten decides that they should get a set from the Fabulös range – little tumblers which taper at the base and have two blobs of swirling blue and purple across the sides – and then head right home. One of the qualities her husband most admires in her is her decisiveness. But for Rabih, it swiftly becomes evident that the larger, unadorned and straight-sided glasses from the Godis series are the only ones that would really work with the kitchen table.

Romanticism is a philosophy of intuitive agreement. In real love, there is no need tiresomely to articulate or spell things out. When two people belong together, there is simply – at long last – a wondrous reciprocal feeling that both parties see the world in precisely the same way.

'You're really going to like these once we get them home, unpack them and put them next to the plates, I promise. They're just . . . nicer,' says Kirsten, who knows how to be firm when the occasion requires it. To her, the plain tumblers are the sort of thing she associates with school cafeterias and prisons.

'I know what you mean, but I can't help thinking these ones will look cleaner and fresher,' replies Rabih, who is unnerved by anything too decorative.

'Well, we can't stand here discussing it all day,' reasons Kirsten, who has pulled the sleeves of her jumper down over her hands.

'Definitely not,' concurs Rabih.

'So let's just go for the Fabulös and be done with it,' inveighs Kirsten.

'It seems crazy to keep disagreeing, but I genuinely think that would be a bit of a disaster.'

'Thing is, I just have this gut instinct.'

'Likewise,' responds Rabih.

Both equally aware that it would be a genuine waste of time to stand in an aisle at IKEA and argue at length about something as petty as which glasses they should buy (when life is so brief and its real imperatives so huge), with increasing ill-temper, and to the mounting interest of other shoppers, they nonetheless stand in an aisle at IKEA and argue at length about which sort of glasses they should buy. After twenty minutes, with each accusing the other of being a little stupid, they abandon hopes of making a purchase and head back to the car park, Kirsten remarking on the way that she intends to spend the rest of her days drinking out of her cupped hand. For the whole drive home, they stare out of the windscreen without speaking, the silence in the car interrupted only by the occasional clicking of the indicator lights. Dobbie, who has taken to travelling with them, sits daunted in the back seat.

They are serious people. Kirsten is currently at work on a presentation entitled 'Procurement Methods in District Services' which she will be travelling to Dundee next month to deliver in front of an audience of local government officials. Rabih, meanwhile, is the author of a thesis on 'The Tectonics of Space in the Work of Christopher Alexander'. Nevertheless, a surprising number of 'silly things' are constantly cropping up between them. What, for example, is the ideal temperature for a bedroom? Kirsten is convinced that she needs a lot of fresh air at night to keep her head clear and energy levels up the next day. She'd rather the room be a bit cold (and if necessary that she put on an extra jumper or thermal pyjamas) than stuffy and contaminated. The window must stay open. But winters were bitter during Rabih's childhood in Beirut and combating gusts of wind was always taken very seriously (even in a war, his family continued to have strong opinions about draughts). He feels safe somehow, snug and luxurious, when the blinds are down, the curtains are tightly drawn and there's condensation on the inside of the windowpanes.

Or, to consider another point of contention, at what time should they leave the house to go for dinner (a special treat) together on a week night? Kirsten thinks: the reservation is for eight, Origano is approximately three miles away, the journey is normally a short one, but what if there were a hold-up at the main roundabout, like there was last time (when they went to see James and Mairi)? In any event, it wouldn't be a problem to get there a bit early. They could have drink at the bar next door or even take a stroll in the park; they have a lot to catch up on. It would be best to have the cab come by for them at seven. And Rabih thinks: an eight o'clock booking means we can arrive at the restaurant eight fifteen or eight twenty. There are five long emails to deal with before leaving the office and I can't be intimate if there are practical things on my mind. The roads will be clear by then anyway and taxis always come early. We should book the cab for eight.

Or, again, what's the best strategy for telling a story at, let's say, a rather swanky party at the Museum of Scotland, to which they've been invited by a client whom Rabih needs to impress? He believes there are clear rules in force: first establish where the action takes place; then introduce the key participants and sketch out their dilemmas before moving in a quick and direct narrative line to a conclusion (after which it's polite to give someone else, ideally the CEO, who has been waiting patiently, a turn). Kirsten, on the contrary, maintains that it's more engaging to start a story midway through and then track back to the beginning. That way, she feels, the audience gets a more solid sense of what's at stake for the characters. Details add local colour. Not everyone wants to cut right to the chase. And then if the first anecdote seems to go down well, why not throw in a second?

Were their listeners (standing next to a display of a giant stegosaurus whose bones were found in a quarry near Glasgow in the late nineteenth century) to be polled for their opinions, they probably wouldn't express any great objections to either approach; both could be fine, they would affirm. Yet for Kirsten and Rabih themselves, testily recapping the performance as they make their way down to the cloakroom, the divergence feels a great deal more critical and more personal: how, each wonders, can the other understand anything – the world, themselves, their partner – if they are always so random or, at the opposite extreme, always so regimented? But what really adds to the intensity is a new thought that arises whenever a tension comes to light: how can this be endured over a lifetime?

We allow for complexity, and therefore make accommodations for disagreement and its patient resolution, in most of the big areas of life: international trade, immigration, oncology . . . But when it comes to domestic existence, we tend to make a fateful presumption of ease, which in turn inspires in us a tense aversion to protracted negotiation. We would think it peculiar indeed to devote a two-day summit to the management of a bathroom, and positively absurd to hire a professional mediator to help us identify the right time to leave the house to go out for dinner.

'I've married a lunatic,' he thinks, at once scared and self-pitying, as their taxi makes its way at speed through the deserted suburban streets. His partner, no less incensed, sits as far away from him as it is possible to do in the back seat of a taxi. There is no space in Rabih's imagination for the sort of marital discord in which he is presently involved. He is in theory amply prepared for disagreement, dialogue and compromise, but not over such utter stupidity. He's never read or heard of squabbling this bad over such a minor detail. Knowing that Kirsten will be haughty and distant with him possibly until the second course only adds to his agitation. He looks over at the imperturbable driver – an Afghan, to judge from the small plastic flag glued to the dashboard. What must he think of such bickering between two people without poverty or tribal genocide to contend with? Rabih is, in his own eyes, a very kind man who has unfortunately not been allotted the right sorts of issues upon which to exercise his kindness. He would find it so much easier to give blood to an injured child in Badakhshan or to carry water to a family in Kandahar than to lean across and say sorry to his wife.

Not all domestic concerns carry equivalent prestige. One can quickly be made to look a fool for caring a lot about how much noise the other person makes while eating cereal or how long they want to keep magazines for beyond their publication date. It's not difficult to humiliate someone who cleaves to a strict policy on how to stack a dishwasher or how quickly the butter ought to be returned to the fridge after use. When the tensions which bedevil us lack glamour, we are at the mercy of those who might wish to label our concerns petty and odd. We can end up frustrated and at the same time too doubtful of the dignity of our frustrations to have the confidence to outline them calmly for our dubious or impatient audience.

In reality, there are rarely squabbles over 'nothing' in Rabih and Kirsten's marriage. The small issues are really just large ones that haven't been accorded the requisite attention. Their everyday disputes are the loose threads that catch on fundamental contrasts in their personalities.

Were he a keener student of his commitments and disappointments, Rabih might (in relation to the air temperature) have explained, from under the duvet, 'When you say you want a window open in the middle of winter, it scares and upsets me – emotionally rather than physically. It seems to me to speak of a future in which precious things will be trampled upon. It reminds me of a certain sadistic stoicism and cheerful bravery in you which I am generally in flight from. On some subconscious level, I feel afraid that it's not really fresh air you want but that, instead, you'd ideally like to push me out of the window in your charming but brusque, sensible, daunting way.'

And were Kirsten similarly keen to examine her position on punctuality, she might have delivered her own touching oration to Rabih (and the Afghan driver) on the way to the restaurant: 'My insistence on leaving so early is in the end a symptom of fear. In a world of randomness and surprises, it's a technique I've developed to ward off anxiety and an unholy, unnameable sense of dread. I want to be on time the same way others lust for power and from a similar drive for security; it makes a little sense, though only a little, in light of the fact that I spent my childhood waiting for a father who never showed up. It's my own crazy way of trying to stay sane.'

With their respective needs contextualized like this, with each side appreciating the sources of the other's beliefs, a new flexibility might have ensued. Rabih could have suggested setting out for Origano not much past six thirty; and Kirsten might have arranged an airlock for their bedroom.

Without patience for negotiation, there is bitterness: anger that has forgotten where it came from. There is a nagger who wants it done now and can't be bothered to explain why. And there is a naggee who no longer has the heart to explain that his or her resistance is grounded in some sensible counter-arguments or, alternatively, in some touching and perhaps even forgivable flaws of character.

The two parties just hope the problems — so boring to them both — will simply go away.

As it happens, it's in the middle of yet another stand-off about the window and the air temperature that Kirsten's friend Hannah calls from Poland, where she lives with her partner, and asks how 'it', by which she means the marriage (a year old now), is going.

Kirsten's husband has donned an overcoat and woollen hat to maximize the force of his objection to his wife's demands for fresh air and is sitting huddled in childish self-pity in a corner of the room with the duvet over him. She has just referred to him, and not for the first time, as a big jessie.

'Just great,' answers Kirsten.

However fashionable an openness around relationships might be, it remains not a little shameful to have to admit that one just may — despite so many opportunities for reflection and experiment — have gone ahead and married the wrong person.

'I'm here with Rabih, having a quiet night in, catching up on some reading.'

There is in reality no ultimate truth in either Rabih's or Kirsten's mind as to how things actually are between them. Their lives involve a constant rotation of moods. Over a single weekend, they might spin from claustrophobia to admiration, desire to boredom, indifference to ecstasy, irritation to tenderness. To arrest the wheel at any one point in order to share a candid verdict with a third party would be to risk being held for ever to a confession which might, with hindsight, turn out to reflect only a momentary state of mind – gloomy pronouncements always commanding an authority that happier ones can't trump.

So long as they keep making sure there are no witnesses to their struggles, Kirsten and Rabih are free not to have to decide quite how well or how badly things are going between them.

The ordinary challenging relationship remains a strangely and unhelpfully neglected topic. It's the extremes that repeatedly grab the spotlight — the entirely blissful partnerships or the murderous catastrophes — and so it is hard to know what we should make of, and how lonely we should feel about, such things as immature rages, late-night threats of divorce, sullen silences, slammed doors and everyday acts of thoughtlessness and cruelty.

Ideally, art would give us the answers that other people don't. This might even be one of the main points of literature: to tell us what society at large is too prudish to explore. The important books should be those that leave us wondering, with relief and gratitude, how the author could possibly have known so much about our lives.

But too often a realistic sense of what an endurable relationship is ends up weakened by silence, societal or artistic. We hence imagine that things are far worse for us than they are for other couples. Not only are we unhappy; we misunderstand how freakish and rare our particular form of unhappiness might be. We end up believing that our struggles are indications of having made some unusual and fundamental error, rather than evidence that our marriages are essentially going entirely according to plan.

They are spared continuous bitterness by two reliable curatives. The first is poor memory. It is hard, by four o'clock on a Thursday afternoon, to remember quite what the fury in the taxi the previous evening was really about. Rabih knows it had something to do with Kirsten's slightly contemptuous tone, combined with the flippant, ungrateful way she responded to his remark about having to leave work early for no good reason, but the precise contours of the offence have now lost their focus, thanks to the sunlight that came through the curtains at six in the morning, the chatter on the radio about ski resorts, a full inbox, the jokes over lunch, the preparations for the conference and the two-hour meeting about the website's design, which together have gone almost as far towards patching things up between them as a mature, direct discussion would have done.

The second remedy is more abstract: it can be difficult to remain furious for very long given quite how large the universe happens to be. A few hours after the IKEA incident, around mid-afternoon, Rabih and Kirsten set off on a long-planned walk in the Lammermuir Hills to the southeast of Edinburgh. They start out silent and cross, but nature gradually releases them from the grip of their mutual indignation, not through its sympathy but through its sublime indifference. Stretching interminably far into the distance, created through the compression of sedimentary rocks in the Ordovician and Silurian periods (some 500 million years before IKEA was founded), the hills strongly suggest that the struggle which has lately loomed so large in their minds does not in fact occupy such a significant place in the cosmic order and is as nothing when set against the aeons of time to which the landscape attests. Clouds drift across the horizon without pausing to take stock of their injured sense of pride. Nothing and no one seem to care: not the family of common sandpipers circling up ahead, the curlew, the snipe, the golden plover or the meadow pipit. Not the honeysuckle, the foxgloves or the harebells, nor the three sheep near Fellcleugh Wood that are grazing on a rare patch of clover with grave intent. Having felt belittled by each other for most of the day, Rabih and

Kirsten are now relieved from feeling small by an apprehension of the vastness within which their lives unfold. They become readier to laugh off their own insignificance as it is pointed out to them by forces indomitably more powerful and impressive than they are.

So helpful are the limitless horizon and ancient hills that by the time they reach a café in the village of Duns, they have even forgotten what they are meant to be furious with each other about. Two cups of tea later, they have agreed to drive back to IKEA, where they eventually manage to pick out some glasses that they will both succeed in tolerating for the rest of their lives: twelve tumblers from the Svalka range.

Sulks

For a good while, everyone else feels superfluous to them. They don't want to see any of the friends on whom they each depended in the long years before their meeting. But then guilt and a renewed curiosity gradually get the better of them. In practice this means seeing more of Kirsten's friends, as Rabih's are scattered around the world. Kirsten's Aberdeen University gang congregate in the Bow Bar on Fridays. It's way across town from their flat but it offers a great range of whiskies and craft beers – although, on the night Kirsten persuades Rabih to visit, he settles for a sparkling water. It's not because of his religion specifically, he has to explain (five times); he's just not really in the mood for a drink.

' "Husband and wife", wow!' says Catherine, a trace of mockery in her voice. She is against marriage and responds best to people who confirm her bias. Of course, the phrase 'husband and wife' still sounds a bit odd to Rabih and Kirsten as well. They likewise often place the titles in ironic quotation marks to mitigate their weight and incongruity, for they don't feel anything like the sort of people they tend to associate with the words, which evoke characters far older, more established and more miserable than they take themselves to be. 'Mrs Khan is here,' Kirsten likes to call out when she comes home, playing with a concept that remains only distantly believable to either of them.

'So, Rabih, where do you work?' asks Murray, who is gruff, bearded, in the oil industry and a one-time admirer of Kirsten's at university.

'At an urban design firm,' Rabih tells him, and feels distinctly like a girl, as he does sometimes in the presence of more solid males. 'We do civic spaces and spatial zoning.'

'Hang on, mate,' says Murray, 'you've lost me already.'

'He's an architect,' Kirsten clarifies. 'He's done houses and offices as well. And hopefully he'll do more when the economy picks up again.'

'I see – sitting out the recession in these dark parts of the kingdom, are we, before bursting back into the limelight to put up the next Great Pyramid of Giza?'

Murray chortles a bit too loudly at his own unfunny jibe, but it's not this that bothers Rabih; rather, it's the way Kirsten joins in, cradling in her hand what remains of her pint, inclining her head towards her old college buddy and laughing heartily along with him, as though something quite amusing really has been said.

Rabih stays quiet on the way home, then claims he's tired, answers with the famous 'Nothing' when asked what's wrong and, once they are inside the flat, which still smells of fresh paint, heads into the den with the sofa bed in it and slams the door shut behind him.

'Oh, come on!' she says, raising her voice to be heard. 'At least tell me what's going on.'

To which he replies, 'Fuck you. Leave me alone.' Which is sometimes how fear can sound.

Kirsten brews herself some tea, then goes to the bedroom, insisting to herself – not entirely truthfully – that she has no idea what her new husband (who truly did look an odd sight in the Bow Bar) can possibly be so upset about.

At the heart of a sulk lies a confusing mixture of intense anger and an equally intense desire not to communicate what one is angry about. The sulker both desperately needs the other person to understand and yet remains utterly committed to doing nothing to help them do so. The very need to explain forms the kernel of the insult: if the partner requires an explanation, he or she is clearly not worthy of one. We should add that it is a privilege to be the recipient of a sulk: it means the other person respects and trusts us enough to think we should understand their un-spoken hurt. It is one of the odder gifts of love.

Eventually she gets out of bed and knocks at the door of the den. Her mother always said one should never go to bed on an argument. She is still telling herself that she does not under-stand what's up. 'Darling, you're behaving as if you were two years old. I'm on your side, remember? At least explain what's wrong.'

And inside the narrow room crammed with books about archi-tecture, the oversized toddler turns over on the sofa bed and can think of nothing beyond the fact that he will not relent – that and, irrelevantly, how strange seem the words stamped in silver foil along the spine of a book on a nearby shelf: MIES VAN DER ROHE.

It's an unusual situation for him to be in. He always tried very hard, in past relationships, to be the one who cared a little less, but Kirsten's buoyancy and steeliness have cast him in the opposite role. It's his turn now to lie awake and fret. Why did all her friends hate him? What does she see in them? Why didn't she step in to help and defend him?

Sulking pays homage to a beautiful, dangerous ideal that can be traced back to our earliest childhoods: the promise of wordless understanding. In the womb, we never had to explain. Our every requirement was catered for. The right sort of comfort simply happened. Some of this idyll continued in our first years. We didn't have to make our needs known: large, kind people guessed for us. They saw past our tears, our inarticulacy, our confusions; they found the explanations for discomforts which we lacked the ability to verbalize.

That may be why, in relationships, even the most eloquent among us may instinctively prefer not to spell things out when our partners are at risk of failing to read us properly. Only wordless and accurate mind-reading can feel like a true sign that our partner is someone to be trusted; only when we don't have to explain can we feel certain that we are genuinely understood.

When he can't bear it any longer, he tiptoes into their bedroom and sits on her side of the bed. He is planning to wake her up but thinks better of it when he sees her intelligent, kind face at rest. Her mouth is slightly open and he can hear the faintest sound of her breathing; the fine hairs on her arm are visible in the light from the street.

It's cool but sunny the next morning. Kirsten gets up before Rabih and prepares two soft-boiled eggs, one for each of them, along with a basket of neatly cut soldiers. She looks down at the willow tree in the garden and feels grateful for the dependable, modest, everyday things. When Rabih enters the kitchen, sheepish and dishevelled, they start off in silence, then end up by smiling at each other. At lunchtime he sends her an email: 'I'm a bit mad. Forgive me.' Although she's waiting to go into a council meeting, she replies swiftly: 'It would be v. boring if you weren't. And lonely.' The sulk is not mentioned again.

We would ideally remain able to laugh, in the gentlest way, when we are made the special target of a sulker's fury. We would recognize the touching paradox. The sulker may be six foot one and holding down adult employment, but the real message is poignantly retrogressive: 'Deep inside, I remain an infant, and right now I need you to be my parent. I need you correctly to guess what is truly ailing me, as people did when I was a baby, when my ideas of love were first formed.'

We do our sulking lovers the greatest possible favour when we are able to regard their tantrums as we would those of an infant. We are so alive to the idea that it's patronizing to be thought of as younger than we are, we forget that it is also, at times, the greatest privilege for someone to look beyond our adult self in order to engage with — and forgive — the disappointed, furious, inarticulate child within.

Sex and Censorship

They're in a café they sometimes go to on a Saturday morning, ordering scrambled eggs, catching up on the week and reading the papers. Today Kirsten is telling Rabih about the dilemma faced by her friend Shona, whose boyfriend, Alasdair, has abruptly been relocated to Singapore for work. Should she follow him there, Shona wonders (they've been together two years), or stay in the dental surgery in Inverness, where she's only just been promoted? It's a pretty weighty decision by any measure. But Kirsten's exegesis is proceeding rather slowly and not always linearly, so Rabih also keeps an eye on the events covered by the *Daily Record*. Some peculiar and macabre situations have been unfolding recently in venues with highly lyrical place-names: a history supply teacher has beheaded his wife with an ancient sword in a house outside Lochgelly, while in Auchtermuchty police are searching for a fifty-four-year-old man who fathered a child with his sixteen-year-old daughter.

'Mr Khan, if you don't stop thinking that everything I tell you is merely background noise which you can shut out at will, I promise you that what happened to that poor woman in Lochgelly will come to seem to you like a day at Disneyland,' says Kirsten, who then jabs him hard in the ribs with a (blunt) knife.

But it isn't just the case of incest in Fife and Shona's predicament that are preoccupying Rabih. There's a third claim on his attention as well. Angelo and Maria have owned their café for thirty years. Angelo's father, originally from Sicily, was a detainee in the Orkney Islands during the Second World War. The couple have a twenty-one-year-old daughter, Antonella, who has lately graduated (with distinction) from her course in catering and hospitality at North East Scotland College in Aberdeen. Until something more substantial turns up, she's helping out in the café, rushing back and forth between the kitchen and the seating area, carrying as many as four orders at a time, issuing constant warnings that the plates are very hot as she manoeuvres gracefully among the tables. She's tall, strong, good-natured – and extremely beautiful. She chats easily with the patrons about the weather and, with some of the regulars who have known her since she was a girl, about the newest developments in her life. She's single right now, she informs a couple of animated elderly ladies at the table opposite, adding that she genuinely doesn't mind – and saying no, she'd never try one of those internet dating things, that's not her style. She is wearing a surprisingly large crucifix on a chain around her neck.

As Rabih watches her, and without quite meaning for it to happen, one part of his mind leaves behind its normal responsibilities and starts to conjure a sequence of wayward images: the narrow stairs behind the espresso machine which lead up to the flat above; Antonella's small room, cluttered with still-unpacked boxes from college; a shaft of morning light catching her jet-black hair and throwing her pale skin into relief; her clothes discarded in a pile by the chair and Antonella herself lying on the bed with her long, muscular legs spread wide open, wholly naked apart from the crucifix.

In the West, we owe to Christianity the view that sex should only ever rightly occur in the presence of love. The religion insists that two people who care for each other must reserve their bodies, and their gaze, for each other alone. To think sexually about strangers is to abandon the true spirit of love and to betray God and one's own humanity.

Such precepts, at once touching and forbidding, have not entirely evaporated along with the decline of the faith that once supported them. Shorn of their explicitly theistic rationale, they seem to have been absorbed into the ideology of Romanticism, which accords a similarly prestigious place to the concept of sexual fidelity within the idea of love. In the secular world, too, monogamy has been declared a necessary and crowning expression of emotional commitment and virtue. Our age has strikingly maintained the essential drift of an earlier religious position: the belief that true love must entail wholehearted sexual fidelity.

Rabih and Kirsten head home, walking slowly, hand in hand, occasionally stopping to browse in a shop. It's going to be a remarkably warm day and the sea looks turquoise, almost tropical. It's Kirsten's turn to go first in the shower, and when they're both done, they go back to bed feeling that, after a long and hard week, they deserve to indulge themselves.

They love to make up stories during sex. One of them will kick off, then the other will take it forward and pass it back for further elaboration. The scenarios can get extreme. 'It's after school and the classroom is empty,' Kirsten begins one time. 'You've asked me to stay behind so we can go over my essay. I'm shy and blush easily, a legacy of my strict Catholic upbringing . . .' Rabih adds details: 'I'm the geography teacher, specializing in glaciers. My hands are shaking. I touch your left knee, hardly daring to believe that . . .'

So far, they have co-authored stories featuring a lost male

mountaineer and a resourceful female doctor, their friends Mike and Bel, and a pilot and her reserved but curious passenger. There is nothing structurally unusual, therefore, in Rabih's impulse, this morning, to initiate a narrative involving a waitress, a crucifix and a leather strap.

Although it often struggles to be heard in respectable circles, there is an alternative to the Christian-Romantic tenet that sex and love should always be inseparable. The libertine position denies any inherent or logical link between loving someone and needing to be unfailingly sexually loyal to them. It proposes that it can be entirely natural and even healthy for partners in a couple occasionally to have sex with strangers for whom they have little feeling but to whom they nonetheless feel strongly attracted. Sex doesn't always have to be bound up with love. It can sometimes – this philosophy holds – be a purely physical, aerobic activity engaged in without substantive emotional meaning. It is, so its adherents conclude, just as absurd to suppose that one should only ever have sex with the person one loves as it would be to require that only those in committed couples ever be permitted to play table tennis or go jogging together.

This remains, in the current age, the minority view by a very wide margin.

Rabih sets the scene: 'So we're in this little seaside town in Italy, maybe Rimini, and we've had some ice cream, maybe pistachio, when you notice the waitress, who is shy but really friendly in a natural way that's at once maternal and fascinatingly virginal.'

'You mean Antonella.'

'Not necessarily.'

'Rabih Khan, shut up!' Kirsten scoffs.

'OK, then – Antonella. So we suggest to Antonella that after she's finished her shift, she might want to come back to our hotel for some grappa. She's flattered but a bit embarrassed. You see, she's got a boyfriend, Marco, a mechanic at the local garage, who's very jealous but at the same time remarkably incompetent sexually. There are certain things that she's been wanting to have a go at for ages but that he flat out refuses to try. She can't get them out of her head, which is in part why she takes us up on our unusual offer.'

Kirsten is silent.

'Now we're in the hotel, in the room, which has a big bed with an old-fashioned brass headboard. Her skin is so soft. There's a trace of moisture on the down of her upper lip. You lick it off, and then your hand moves gently down her body.' Rabih continues: 'She's still wearing her apron, which you help her out of. You find her sweet, but you also want to use her in a rather mercenary way. That's where the strap comes in. You slide her bra up — it's black, or no, maybe grey — and lean over to take one of her breasts in your mouth. Her nipples are hard.'

Still Kirsten says nothing.

'You reach down and slip your hand inside her particularly lacy Italian panties,' he goes on. 'Suddenly you feel you want to lick her between her legs, so you get her up on all fours and begin to explore her from behind.'

By now the silence from Rabih's usual storytelling partner has grown oppressive.

'Are you OK?' he asks.

'I'm fine, it's just . . . I don't know . . . it feels weird for you to be thinking about Antonella that way — a bit perverted, really. She's such a lovely person. I've known her since she was sitting her Highers, and now her parents are so proud of the distinction she got. I don't like the old chestnut of the man sitting there getting off on watching two women licking each other out. Sfouf, it feels, frankly, sort of stupid and porno. As for the anal thing, to be honest –'

'I'm sorry, you're right, it's ridiculous,' interrupts Rabih, suddenly feeling utterly daft. 'Let's forget I ever said anything. We shouldn't let something like this come between us and the Brioschi Café.'

Romanticism hasn't only increased the prestige of monogamous sex; along the way it has also made any extraneous sexual interest seem unvaryingly foolish and unkind. It has powerfully redefined the meaning of the urge to sleep with someone other than one's regular partner. It has turned every extramarital interest into a threat and, often, something close to an emotional catastrophe.

In fantasy in Rabih's mind, it could have been such a tender and easy transaction. He and Kirsten would have chatted with Antonella in the café, all three of them would have recognized the tension and the appeal and then in short order they would have ended up back at Merchiston Avenue. Antonella and Kirsten would have made out for a while as he looked on from an armchair, then he would have taken Kirsten's place and had sex with Antonella. It would have felt warm, exciting and wholly meaningless in terms of the marriage and of Rabih's essential love for Kirsten. Afterwards he would have walked Antonella back to the café, and none of them would ever have mentioned the interlude again. There would have been no melodrama, no possessiveness and no guilt. At Christmas they might have bought her a panettone and a card by way of thanks for the orgy.

Despite the liberal atmosphere of our time, it would be naive to assume that the distinction between 'weird' and 'normal' has disappeared. It stands as secure as ever, waiting to intimidate and herd back into line those who would question the normative limits of love and sex. It may now be deemed 'normal' to wear cut-off shorts, expose bellybuttons, marry someone of either gender and watch a little porn for fun, but it also remains indispensably 'normal' to believe that true love should be monogamous and that one's desire should be focused exclusively on one person. To be in dispute with this founding principle is to risk being dismissed, in public or private, with that most dispiriting, caustic and shameful of all epithets: pervert.

Rabih belongs firmly outside the category of the good communicators. For all that he nurses some strongly held views, he has long found the journey towards expressing these fraught with obstacles and inhibitions. When his boss, Ewen, announces a new corporate strategy of concentrating more on the oil sector and less on local government contracts, Rabih doesn't – as someone else might do – request a meeting and sit down with him for half an hour in the top-floor conference room with its view over Calton Hill to explain why this policy shift could prove not only mistaken but possibly dangerous. Instead he remains largely quiet, making only a few gnomic remarks and fantasizing that others will somehow magically deduce his opinion. Similarly, when he realizes that Gemma, an entry-level staffer who has been taken on to assist him with his workload, has been getting many of her measurements wrong, he feels inwardly frustrated but never raises the issue with her and simply does the work himself, leaving the young woman amazed by how little there is for her to do in her new job. He's not secretive, controlling or withdrawn for malicious reasons; he just gives up on other people – and on his ability to persuade them of anything – with unhelpful ease.

For the rest of the day, after their visit to the Brioschi Café and the humiliating business about Antonella, there's the kind of tension between Rabih and Kirsten that often follows on from aborted sex. Somewhere in his mind Rabih feels a disappointment and irritation that he doesn't know what to do with. After all, it isn't right to start making a fuss when your partner isn't wild at the idea of having a threesome with a recent graduate who knows her way around a plate of eggs and happens to look nice in an apron.

What makes people good communicators is, in essence, an ability not to be fazed by the more problematic or offbeat aspects of their own characters. They can contemplate their anger, their sexuality and their unpopular, awkward or unfashionable opinions without losing confidence or collapsing into self-disgust. They can speak clearly because they have managed to develop a priceless sense of their own acceptability. They like themselves well enough to believe that they are worthy of and can win the goodwill of others, if only they have the wherewithal to present themselves with the right degree of patience and imagination.

As children, these good communicators must have been blessed with caregivers who knew how to love their charges without demanding that every last thing about them be agreeable and perfect. Such parents would have been able to live with the idea that their offspring might sometimes — for a while, at least — be odd, violent, angry, mean, peculiar or sad, and yet still deserve a place within the circle of familial love. The parents would thus have created an invaluable wellspring of courage from which those children would eventually be able to draw to sustain the confessions and direct conversations of adult life.

Rabih's father was taciturn and severe. Only one generation removed from a life of extreme poverty and agricultural labour in a small village near Baalbek, he had been the first in his family to escape and go to university, though he would continue to preserve a long ancestral legacy of being careful around authority. Speaking up and volunteering one's opinions were not standard practices among the Khans.

The education in communication imparted by Rabih's mother was no more encouraging. She loved him fiercely, but she needed him to be a certain way. Whenever she returned from her airline work to the anxious atmosphere of Beirut and of her marriage, her son would see the strain around her eyes and feel that he mustn't add to her problems. He wanted more than anything to put her at ease and make her laugh. Whatever anxieties he felt, he would reflexively conceal. His job was to help keep her intact. He could not afford to tell her too many tricky but true things about himself.

Rabih thereby grew up to understand the love of others as a reward for being good, not for being transparent. As an adult and as a husband, he lacks any idea of how to make something coherent out of the non-normative parts of himself. It is neither arrogance nor a sense that his wife has no right to know who he really is that makes him secretive and hesitant; rather, it is sheer terror that his tendencies towards self-loathing will be intensified to an unbearable degree by the presence of a witness.

Were Rabih less afraid of his own mind, he might be able to square up to Kirsten with his desires, like a natural scientist holding up for a colleague's inspection some newly discovered, peculiar-looking species which both of them might strive to understand and accommodate themselves to. But he instinctively feels that there is quite a lot about himself that it would be wiser for him not to share. He is too dependent on Kirsten's love to map out for her all the places to which his libido regularly takes him. She thus never learns about the woman her husband daily admires behind the till at the newsagent's in Waverley Station, or his curiosity about her friend Rachel on the night of her birthday, or the dress that turns him on in a shop on Hanover Street, or some of his thoughts about stockings, or some of the faces that, unbidden, occasionally pass through his mind while he is in bed with her.

The first heady period of sexual adventure and total honesty passes. It is significantly more important to Rabih now that he remains attractive to Kirsten than that he is a truthful correspondent of the reality of his inner life.

Good listeners are no less rare or important than good communicators. Here, too, an unusual degree of confidence is the key – a capacity not to be thrown off course by, or buckle under the weight of, information that may deeply challenge certain settled assumptions. Good listeners are unfussy about the chaos which others may for a time create in their minds; they've been there before and know that everything can eventually be set back in its place.

The blame is not on Rabih's side alone. In having on the tip of her tongue such words as *weird* and *perverted*, Kirsten does little to foster an atmosphere ripe for revelations. Then again, she uses these words not out of nastiness or contempt but rather out of fear that by tacitly endorsing Rabih's fantasies she may end up giving them greater licence and so undermine their love.

She might instead, in another mood, as a different person, have said something like the following in response to her husband's scenario: 'The nature of this particular daydream is foreign, unfamiliar and frankly not a little disgusting to me, but I'm interested in hearing about it nonetheless, because more critical than my relative comfort is my ability to cope with who you are. The person thinking of Antonella just now is the same person I married in Inverness and the same little boy who stares out from that picture on top of our chest of drawers. It's him I love and refuse to think badly of, however much his thoughts may sometimes disturb me. You're my best friend, and I want to know and come to terms with your mind in all its weird byways. I will never be able to do or be everything you want, nor vice versa, but I'd like to think we can be the sort of people who will dare to tell each other who we really are. The alternative is silence and lies, which are the real enemies of love.'

Or conversely, she might have revealed the vulnerability that has lain all the while behind her annoyed demeanour: 'I wish I could be everything to you. I wish you didn't have such needs outside of me. Of course, I don't really think your fantasies about Antonella are repulsive; I just wish there didn't have to be — always — that imagined someone else. I know it's madness, but what I want most is to be able to satisfy you all by myself.'

In the event, Rabih didn't speak, and Kirsten didn't listen. Instead they went to the cinema and had a thoroughly nice evening together. In the engine room of their relationship, however, a warning light had come on.

It is precisely when we hear little from our partner which frightens, shocks or sickens us that we should begin to be concerned, for this may be the surest sign that we are being gently lied to or shielded from the other's imagination, whether out of kindness or from a touching fear of losing our love. It may mean that we have, despite ourselves, shut our ears to information that fails to conform to our hopes, hopes which will thereby be endangered all the more.

Rabih resigns himself to being partially misunderstood — and, unconsciously, to blaming his wife for not accepting those sides of his nature that he lacks the courage to explain to her. Kirsten, for her part, settles for never daring to ask her husband what is really going on in his sexual mind outside of her role in it, and chooses not to look very hard at why it is that she feels so afraid to find out more.

As for the raven-haired subject of Rabih's fantasy, her name doesn't come up in conversation again for a long while, until one day Kirsten returns from having a coffee at the Brioschi Café with some news. Antonella has moved up north to work as the head receptionist at a small luxury hotel in Argyll, on the western coast, and has fallen deeply in love with one of the housekeepers there, a young Dutch woman, to whom — much to her parents' initial surprise but also eventual delight — she plans to get married in a few months' time in a big ceremony in the town of Apeldoorn, information that Rabih receives with an almost convincing show of complete indifference. He has chosen love over libido.

Transference

Two years into their marriage, Rabih's job remains precarious, vulnerable to an unsteady workflow and clients' sudden changes of mind. So he feels especially pleased when, at the start of January, the firm wins a large and long-term contract across the border in England, in South Shields, a struggling town two and a half hours southeast of Edinburgh by train. The task is to redevelop the quayside and a derelict hodgepodge of industrial sheds into a park, a café and a museum to house a local maritime artefact, the *Tyne*, the second-oldest lifeboat in Britain. Ewen asks Rabih if he will head up the project, a distinct honour, yet one which also means that for half a year he will have to spend three nights a month away from Kirsten. The budget is tight, so he makes his base in South Shields's Premier Inn, a modestly priced establishment sandwiched between a women's prison and a goods yard. In the evenings he has supper by himself at the hotel restaurant, Taybarns, where a side of gammon sweats under the lamps of a carving station.

During his second visit there, the local officials prevaricate on a range of issues. Everyone is too terrified to make big decisions and delays are blamed on assorted incomprehensible regulations; it's a miracle they have even managed to get this far. There's a vein in Rabih's neck that throbs at such moments. Shortly after nine, pacing the nylon carpet in his socks, he calls Kirsten from his maroon and purple room. 'Teckle,' he greets her. 'Another day of mind-numbing meetings and idiots from the council causing trouble for no good reason. I miss you so much. I'd pay a lot for a hug from you right now.' There's a pause (he feels that he can hear the miles that separate them), then she replies in a flat voice that he has to get his name added to the car insurance before 1 March, adding that their neighbour also wants to speak to them about the drain, the one on the garden side – at which point Rabih repeats, gently but firmly, that he misses her and wishes they could be together. In Edinburgh, Kirsten is curled up at one end, 'his' end, of the sofa, wearing his jumper, with a bowl of tuna and a slice of toast on her lap. She pauses again, but when she responds to Rabih, it is with a curt and administrative-sounding 'Yes'. It's a pity he can't see that she is fighting back tears.

It isn't the first such instance. Something similarly frosty happened the last time he was here, and once when he was in Denmark for a conference. Then, he accused her of being odd on the phone. Now, he is simply hurt. He only made a reasonable plea for warmth and suddenly they seem to be in a stalemate. He looks out at the prison windows opposite. Whenever he's away, he feels as if she were trying to put an even greater distance between them than that of land or water. He wishes he could find a way to reach her and wonders what could have caused her to become so remote and unavailable. Kirsten isn't quite sure herself. She is looking with watery eyes at the bark of an old weathered tree just beyond the window, thinking with particular concentration about a file she'll have to remember to take to work tomorrow.

The structure looks something like this: an apparently ordinary situation or remark elicits from one member of a couple a reaction that doesn't seem quite warranted, being unusually full of annoyance or anxiety, irritability or coldness, panic or recrimination. The person on the receiving end is puzzled: after all, it was just a simple request for a loving goodbye, a plate or two left unwashed in the sink, a small joke at the other's expense or a few minutes' delay. Why, then, the peculiar and somehow outsized response?

The behaviour makes little sense when one tries to understand it according to the current facts. It's as if some aspect of the present scenario were drawing energy from another source, as if it were unwittingly triggering a pattern of behaviour that the other person originally developed long ago, in order to meet a particular threat, which has now somehow been subconsciously re-evoked. The overreactor is responsible, as the psychological term puts it, for the 'transference' of an emotion from the past on to someone in the present — who perhaps doesn't entirely deserve it.

Our minds are, oddly, not always good at knowing what era they are in. They jump a little too easily, like an erstwhile victim of burglary who keeps a gun by the bed and is startled awake by every rustle.

What's worse for the loved ones standing in the vicinity is that people in the throes of a transference have no easy way of knowing, let alone calmly explaining, what they are up to; they simply feel that their response is entirely appropriate to the occasion. Their partners, on the other hand, may reach a rather different and rather less flattering conclusion: that they are distinctly odd — and maybe even a little mad.

Kirsten's father leaves her when she is seven. He walks out of the house without warning or explanation. On the very day before he goes, he plays at being a camel on the living-room floor and carries her on his back around the sofa and armchairs. At bedtime he reads to her from a book of German folk tales, those stories of lonely children and wicked stepmothers, of magic and of loss. He tells her they are only stories. And then he disappears.

There could have been many responses. Hers is not to feel. She can't afford to. She is doing so well, that's what everyone says – the teachers, her two aunts, the counsellor she sees for a time. Her schoolwork actually improves. But she's not even remotely coping inside: it takes a certain strength to cry, the confidence that one will eventually be able to staunch the tears. She doesn't have the luxury of feeling just a little sad. The danger is that she might fall apart and never know how to put the pieces back together. To prevent the possibility she cauterizes her wounds, as best she can, aged seven.

She can now love (in her own way), but what she really can't countenance is missing someone too much, not even if the person is only in a town a couple of hours to the southeast and is most definitely going to be returning home in a few days on the 18.22 train.

But of course, she can't explain or even quite grasp this habit of hers. It doesn't make her popular at home. She would ideally have in her employ a guardian spirit with magical powers to pause the action just as Rabih begins to get annoyed, in order then to whisk him out of his budget hotel and bear him aloft, through the dense clouds of the lower atmosphere, to the Inverness of a quarter-century before, where he could peer through the window of a little house and into the narrow bedroom in which a small girl in bear pyjamas is sitting at her desk, colouring in squares on a large piece of paper with methodical precision, trying to hold on to her sanity, her mind blank from a sadness too overwhelming to admit.

If Rabih were presented with this picture of Kirsten's stoic endurance, compassion would come naturally to him. He would understand the touching reasons for her reserve and would immediately quell his own hurt so as to offer her tender reassurance and sympathy.

But as there is no spirit waiting in the wings, and therefore no stirring sensory narrative cued up to illuminate Kirsten's past, Rabih has only her affectless response to try to make sense of – a challenge that inspires in him a predictably irresistible temptation to judge and to take offence.

We too often act from scripts generated by the crises of long ago that we've all but consciously forgotten. We behave according to an archaic logic which now escapes us, following a meaning we can't properly lay bare to those we depend on most. We may struggle to know which period of our lives we are really in, with whom we are truly dealing and what sort of behaviour the person before us is rightfully owed. We can be a little tricky to be around.

Rabih is not so different from his wife. He, too, constantly interprets the present through the distortions of his past and is moved by obsolete and eccentric impulses which he cannot explain to himself or to Kirsten.

What does it mean, for example, to come home from the office in Edinburgh and find a big pile of clothes in the hall, which Kirsten planned to take to the dry-cleaner's but then forgot about and says she will get around to sometime in the next few days?

There's one swift and leading answer for Rabih: that this is the onset of the chaos he fears and that Kirsten may have done this specifically to unnerve and wound him. Unable to follow her advice to leave the pile until the next day, he takes the clothes out himself (it's seven at night) and then, on his return, spends half an hour noisily cleaning up the rest of the flat, paying particular attention to the muddle in the cutlery drawer.

'The chaos' is no small matter in Rabih's mind. All too quickly his unconscious draws a connection between minor things that are out of place in the present and very major things that were once out of place in the past, such as the scarred hulk of the InterContinental Phoenicia Hotel that he used to see from his bedroom; the bombed-out American Embassy that he walked past every morning; the murderous graffiti that routinely appeared on the wall of his school; and the late-night shouting he would hear between his mother and father. With complete clarity, he still sees, today, the black outline of the Cypriot refugee ship that finally took him and his parents out of the city on a dark January night, and the apartment that they later heard had been looted and now housed a family of Druze fighters (his room reportedly serving as an ammunition dump). There is a good deal of history in his hysteria.

In the present, Rabih may be living in one of the safer, quieter corners of the globe, with a wife who is fundamentally kind and committedly on his side, but in his mind Beirut, war and the cruellest sides of human nature remain threats forever just out of his line of sight, always ready to colour his interpretation of the meaning of a pile of clothes or an organizational erosion in the cutlery drawer.

When our minds are involved in transference, we lose the ability to give people and things the benefit of the doubt; we swiftly and anxiously move towards the worst conclusions that the past once mandated.

Unfortunately, to admit that we may be drawing on the confusions of the past to force an interpretation on to what's happening now seems humbling and not a little humiliating: surely we know the difference between our partner and a disappointing parent, between a husband's short delay and a father's permanent abandonment, between some dirty laundry and a civil war?

The business of repatriating emotions emerges as one of the most delicate and necessary tasks of love. To accept the risks of transference is to prioritize sympathy and understanding over irritation and judgement. Two people can come to see that sudden bursts of anxiety or hostility may not always be directly caused by them – and so should not always be met with fury or wounded pride. Bristling and condemnation can give way to compassion.

By the time Rabih gets back from his trip to England, Kirsten has reverted to some of the habits she indulged in when she lived on her own. She's drunk a beer while having a bath and eaten cereal from a mug in bed. But soon enough their mutual desire and capacity for closeness reassert themselves. The reconciliation starts, as it often does, with a little joke which puts its finger on the underlying anxiety.

'Sorry to have interrupted you, Mrs Khan, but I think I used to live here,' says Rabih.

'Definitely not. You must be looking for 34A and this is 34*B*, you see . . .'

'I think we once got married. Do you remember? That's our child, Dobbie, over there in the corner. He's very silent. Kind of like his mum.'

'I'm sorry, Rabih,' says Kirsten, turning serious. 'I'm a bit of a bitch when you go away. I seem to be trying to punish you for leaving me, which is ridiculous because you're only trying to pay off our mortgage. Forgive me. I'm a bit of nut-job sometimes.'

Kirsten's words act like an immediate balm. Rabih is flooded with love for his slightly inarticulate and very unself-righteous wife. Her insight is the best welcome-home present she could have given him and the greatest guarantee of the solidity of their love. Neither he nor she has to be perfect, he reflects; they only need to give each other the odd sign they know they can sometimes be quite hard to live with.

We don't need to be constantly reasonable in order to have good relationships; all we need to have mastered is the occasional capacity to acknowledge with good grace that we may, in one or two areas, be somewhat insane.

Universal Blame

For their third wedding anniversary Rabih surprises Kirsten with a weekend trip to Prague. They stay in a little hotel near the Cathedral of Sts Cyril and Methodius, take photos of themselves on the Charles Bridge, talk of life back at home, reflect on how quickly the years are passing and visit the Sternberg Palace to have a look at the early European art. There, Kirsten pauses before a small sixteenth-century Virgin and Child.

'It's so awful what happened to her adorable baby in the end – how could anyone get over that?' she asks pensively. She has an endearing way, Rabih muses, of thinking even the most basic things through afresh for herself. The painting isn't, for her, an object for dutiful academic analysis; instead it's a prefiguring of a parent's most grievous tragedy, and as such, it earns from her a sympathy no less lively or immediate than that she might offer to someone whose son had just died in a motorcycle accident on the road to Fort William.

Kirsten is keen to visit Prague Zoo. It's been a long time since either of them has spent any time around animals, save perhaps for the occasional cat or dog. Their first thought is how very strange all of the inmates look – the camel, for one, with its U-shaped neck, its two furry dorsal pyramids, its eyelashes that might be coated in mascara, and its set of yellow buckteeth. A free brochure gives them some facts: camels can go ten days in the desert without drinking; their humps are filled not with water, as common wisdom holds, but with fat; their eyelashes are designed to shield their eyeballs during sandstorms, and their liver and kidneys extract every drop of moisture possible from the food they eat, causing their dung to be dry and compact.

All animals are distinctive because they have evolved to thrive in very particular environments, the leaflet goes on. That's why the Malagasy giant jumping rat has such big ears and strong hind legs and the redtail catfish of the Amazon sports a camouflaging sandy band across its midriff.

'Of course,' Kirsten interjects, 'but these adaptations aren't much use when your new habitat is actually Prague Zoo, where you're living in a concrete hotel room with a meal delivered to you three times a day through a hatch and there's no entertainment except for the tourists. You just grow fat and tetchy, like the poor sweet melancholic orang-utan, designed for a life in the forests of Borneo and not holding up too well here.'

'But perhaps humans are no different,' adds Rabih, a little put out that a hominid should be receiving so much of his wife's sympathy. 'We're also saddled with impulses which were probably sensible when they evolved on the plains of Africa, yet give us nothing but trouble now.'

'What sorts of things?'

'Being super alert to noises in the night, which now just stops us sleeping when a car alarm goes off. Or being primed to eat anything sweet, which only makes us fat given how many temptations there are. Or feeling almost compelled to look at the legs of strangers in the streets of Prague, which annoys and hurts our partners . . .'

'Mr Khan! Using Darwin to get me to feel sorry for you for not having seven wives and yet another ice cream . . .'

It's late on Sunday evening by the time they finally land, exhausted, at Edinburgh Airport. Kirsten's bag is second off the carousel. Rabih has no such luck, so while they wait, they sit on a bench next to a shuttered sandwich shop. It's unusually warm for the time of year and Kirsten idly wonders what the weather will be like tomorrow. Rabih gets out his phone and checks. A high of 17°C and sunny the entire day: remarkable. Just then he spots his bag on the carousel, goes over to collect it and adds it to their trolley. They board the bus back into the centre of town just before midnight. All around them, similarly worn-out passengers are lost in thought or dozing. Suddenly remembering that he has to send a text to a colleague, Rabih reaches into the right pocket of his jacket for his phone, then looks in the left pocket, then stands up a little in his seat to check the pockets of his trousers.

'Have you got my phone?' he asks Kirsten in an agitated voice. She's sleeping and wakes up with a start.

'Of course not, darling. Why would I take your phone?'

He squeezes past her and reaches up into the overhead rack, takes down his bag and fumbles in the outer compartment. An unfortunate reality gradually becomes clear: the phone has gone missing, and with it his communications system with the world.

'It must have been stolen somewhere in the baggage reclaim,' observes Kirsten. 'Or perhaps you left it behind somehow. Poor you! We can call up the airport first thing tomorrow and find out if anyone has handed it in. But the insurance will cover it anyway. It's sort of amazing this hasn't happened to one of us before.'

But Rabih fails to see the wonder of it.

'You can use my phone if there's anything you want to look at,' adds Kirsten brightly.

Rabih is furious. This is the beginning of an administrative nightmare. He'll be made to wait for hours by a series of operators, then have to dig up paperwork and fill out forms. Oddly enough, though, his fury isn't directed only at his loss; some of it also appears to have found its way to his wife. After all, she was the one who first mentioned the weather, which in turn prompted him to check the forecast, without which the phone might still be safely in his possession. Furthermore, Kirsten's calm and sympathetic manner merely serves to underscore how carefree and lucky she is in comparison. As the bus makes its way towards Waverley Bridge, an important piece of logic falls into place for Rabih: somehow, all the pain and bother and hassle, every bit of it, is her fault. She is to blame for the lot, including the headache that is right now clasping itself like a vice around his temples. He turns away from her and mutters, 'I knew all along we shouldn't have gone on this crazy, unnecessary trip' – which seems a sad and rather unfair way to précis the celebration of an important anniversary.

Not everyone would follow, or sympathize with, the connection Rabih has just made. Kirsten never signed up to the job of guardian of her husband's mobile phone, and is far from responsible for every aspect of this grown primate's life. But to Rabih it makes a curious sort of sense. Not for the first time, everything is, in some way, his wife's doing.

The most superficially irrational, immature, lamentable but nonetheless common of all the presumptions of love is that the person to whom we have pledged ourselves is not just the centre of our emotional existence, but also, as a result and yet in a very strange, objectively insane and profoundly unjust way, responsible for everything that happens to us, for good or ill. Therein lies the peculiar and sick privilege of love.

It has also, over the years, been her 'fault' that he slipped in the snow, that he lost his keys, that the Glasgow train broke down, that he got a speeding fine, that there is an itchy label in his new shirt, that the washing machine isn't draining properly, that he isn't practising architecture to the standard he'd dreamed of, that the new neighbours play music loudly late in the evening and that they hardly ever have much fun any more. And, it should be emphasized, Kirsten's own list is, in this same category, neither any shorter nor any more reasonable: it's all down to Rabih that she doesn't see her mother enough, that her tights constantly ladder, that her friend Gina never gets in touch with her, that she's tired all the time, that the nail clippers have gone missing and that they hardly ever have much fun any more . . .

The world upsets, disappoints, frustrates and hurts us in countless ways at every turn. It delays us, rejects our creative endeavours, overlooks us for promotions, rewards idiots and smashes our ambitions on its bleak, relentless shores. And almost invariably, we can't complain about any of it. It's too difficult to tease out who may really be to blame; and too dangerous to complain even when we know for certain (lest we be fired or laughed at).

There is only one person to whom we can expose our catalogue of grievances, one person who can be the recipient of all our accumulated rage at the injustices and imperfections of our lives. It is of course the height of absurdity to blame them. But this is to misunderstand the rules under which love operates. It is because we cannot scream at the forces who are really responsible that we get angry with those we are sure will best tolerate us for blaming them. We take it out on the very nicest, most sympathetic, most loyal people in the vicinity, the ones least likely to have harmed us, but the ones most likely to stick around while we pitilessly rant at them.

The accusations we direct at our lovers make no particular sense. We would utter such unfair things to no one else on earth. But our wild charges are a peculiar proof of intimacy and trust, a symptom of love itself – and, in their own way, a perverted manifestation of commitment. Whereas we can say something sensible and polite to any stranger, it is only in the presence of the lover we wholeheartedly believe in that we can dare to be extravagantly and boundlessly unreasonable.

A few weeks after their return from Prague, a new and far larger problem arises. Rabih's boss, Ewen, calls a team meeting. After a decent last eight months, the work pipeline is again drying up, he confides. Not everyone currently employed by the firm will be able to stay on board, unless an amazing project turns up soon. In the corridor afterwards, Ewen takes Rabih aside.

'You'll understand, of course,' he says. 'It won't be anything personal. You're a good man, Rabih!' People who are planning to sack you should really have the decency and courage not also to want you to like them, reflects Rabih.

The threat of unemployment plunges him into gloom and anxiety. It would be hell to try to find another job in this city, he knows. He'd probably have to move, and then what would Kirsten do? He is threatening to fail in his most basic responsibilities as a husband. What madness it was, all those years ago, to think he could have a career that would combine financial stability with creative fulfilment. It was a mix of childishness and petulance, as his father always hinted.

Today his walk home takes him past St Mary's Roman Catholic Cathedral. He's never been inside before – the façade has always seemed Gothically gloomy and uninviting – but in his perturbed and panic-stricken mood, he decides to have a look around and ends up in a niche off the nave, in front of a large painting of the Virgin Mary, who gazes down at him with sorrowful and kindly eyes. Something in her sympathetic expression touches him, as if she knew a little about Ewen Frank and the shortage of work and wanted to reassure him of her own ongoing faith in him. He can feel tears coming to his eyes at the contrast between the challenging facts of his adult life and the kindness and tenderness in this woman's expression. She seems to understand and yet not condemn. He is surprised when he looks at his watch and realizes that it's been a quarter of an hour. It's a sort of madness, he concedes, for an atheist of Muslim descent to find himself in a candlelit chapel at the foot of a portrait of a foreign deity to whom he wants to offer his tears and confusion. Still, he has few alternatives, there not being many people left who still believe in him. The main burden of responsibility has fallen on his wife, and that means asking rather a lot of an ordinary, non-canonized mortal.

At home, Kirsten has made a courgette, basil and feta salad for dinner from a recipe of his. She wants to know all the details about the work crisis. When did Ewen tell them this? How did he put it? How did the others react? Will there be another meeting soon? Rabih starts to answer, then snaps.

'Why do you care about these incidental facts? It just is what it is: a big mess.'

He throws down his napkin and starts pacing.

Kirsten wants a blow-by-blow account because that's how she copes with anxiety: she hangs on to, and arranges, the facts. She doesn't want to let on directly quite how worried she is. Her style is to be reserved and focus on the administrative side. Rabih wants to scream or break something. He observes his beautiful, kindly wife – on whom he has become a constant burden. Eight times a year at least they have scenes a little like this, when disasters happen out in the world and Rabih brings them back to the hearth and lays them before Kirsten in a muddled heap.

She joins him where he is standing by the fireplace, takes his hand in hers and says with warmth and sincerity, 'It will be OK' – which they both know isn't necessarily true.

We place such demands on our partners, and become so unreasonable around them, because we have faith that someone who understands obscure parts of us, whose presence solves so many of our woes, must somehow also be able to fix everything about our lives. We exaggerate the other's powers in a curious sort of homage – heard in adult life decades down the line – to a small child's awe at their own parents' apparently miraculous capacities.

To a six-year-old Rabih, his mother seemed almost godlike; she could find his stuffed bear when it was lost, she always made sure that his favourite chocolate milk was in the fridge, she produced fresh clothes for him every morning, she would lie in bed with him and explain why his father had been screaming, she knew how to keep the earth tilted on its correct axis . . .

Both Rabih and Kirsten have learned how to reassure the anxious child selves concealed within their adult partners. That's why they love each other. But they have in the process also unknowingly inherited a little of that dangerous, unfair, beautifully naive trust which little children place in their parents. Some primitive part of the grown-up Rabih and Kirsten insists that the beloved must control far more of the world than any human being in an adult relationship possibly could, which is what generates such anger and frustration when problems nevertheless arise.

Kirsten takes Rabih into her arms. 'If only I could do something, I would,' she says, and Rabih looks sadly and kindly at her, recognizing as if for the first time an essential solitude he is faced with that remains utterly impervious to love. He isn't angry with her; he is panicked and battered by events. To be a better husband, he recognizes, he will have to learn to place a little less of the wrong, destructive sort of hope in the woman who loves him. He must be readier to expect to be, where it counts, all alone.

Teaching and Learning

Rabih's job is saved, though proper security remains elusive. Most of his and Kirsten's friends get married and start to have children, and their social life evolves to become ever more concentrated around other couples. There are half a dozen or so that they see on a regular rotating basis, usually at one another's houses over supper or for lunch (with babies) on the weekend.

There is warmth and companionship among them but also – beneath the surface – a fair amount of comparison and boasting. There are frequent competitive allusions to jobs, holidays, house-improvement plans and the first children's milestones.

Rabih affects a defiant, thick-skinned stance with regard to the jostling and the score-keeping. He frankly concedes to Kirsten that they aren't the highest-status couple, but then quickly adds that it doesn't matter in the least: they should be pleased with what they have. They don't live in a small gossipy village; they can go their own way.

It's almost one in the morning on a Saturday, and they're in the kitchen, clearing up the dishes, when Kirsten remarks that she learned over pudding that Clare and her husband, Christopher, are going to be renting a place in Greece for the whole summer: a villa with its own pool and a garden with a sort of private olive grove. She'll be there all the time, he'll commute down. It sounds out of this world, she says, but it must cost a bloody fortune – unimaginable, really; it's astonishing what a surgeon can earn these days.

For Rabih, the comment niggles. Why does his wife care? Why aren't their own holidays (in a small cottage in the Western Isles) seemingly enough? How could they ever afford anything even approaching the cost of a villa rental on their salaries? This isn't the first such remark she's made in this vein. There was something a week or so ago about a new coat she'd reluctantly had to renounce, then an admiring account of a weekend in Rome that James had invited Mairi on and, only yesterday, an awestruck report about two friends sending their children to private school.

Rabih would love for her to relinquish this tendency. He wants her to take pride in herself without reference to her place in a mean-ingless pecking order, and to appreciate the non-material richness of their life together. He wants her to prize what she has rather than ache for what is missing. But because it's well past his bedtime and this is an inflammatory topic around which he has plenty of his own anxieties, his proposal comes out in a less nuanced and less persuasive form than he might have wished.

'Well, darling, I'm so sorry I'm not a high-rolling surgeon with a villa.' He can hear the sarcasm in his voice, he knows at once the effect it will have, but he cannot stop himself. 'Shame you're stuck here in the slums with me.'

'Why are you having a go at me? And so late as well,' retorts Kirsten. 'I was just saying they're going on holiday, you dober, and immediately, out of nowhere, in the middle of the night, you switch to attacking me – as if you'd been waiting to pounce on me. I remem-ber a time when you weren't always so critical of things I said.'

'I'm not critical. I just care about you.'

The very concept of trying to 'teach' a lover things feels patronizing, incongruous and plain sinister. If we truly loved someone, there could be no talk of wanting him or her to change. Romanticism is clear on this score: true love should involve an acceptance of a partner's whole being. It is this fundamental commitment to benevolence that makes the early months of love so moving. Within the new relationship, our vulnerabilities are treated with generosity. Our shyness, awkwardness and confusion endear (as they did when we were children) rather than generate sarcasm or complaint; the trickier sides of us are interpreted solely through the filter of compassion.

From these moments, a beautiful yet challenging, and even reckless, conviction develops: that to be properly loved must always mean being endorsed for all that one is.

Marriage lends Rabih and Kirsten an opportunity to study each other's characters in exceptional detail. No one in their adult lives has ever had as much time to examine their behaviour in such a constrained habitat and under the influence of so many variable and demanding conditions: late at night and dazed in the morning; despondent and panicked over work; frustrated with friends; in a rage over lost household items.

To this knowledge, they bring ambition for the other's potential. They can at points see important qualities that are lacking but which they believe could be developed if only they were pointed out. They know better than anyone else some of what is wrong – and how it might change. Their relationship is, secretly yet mutually, marked by a project of improvement.

Contrary to appearances, after the dinner party, Rabih is sincerely trying to bring about an evolution in the personality of the wife he loves. But his chosen technique is distinctive: to call Kirsten materialistic, shout at her and then, later, to slam two doors.

'All you seem to care about is how much our friends are earning and how little we have,' he exclaims bitterly to Kirsten, who is by now standing by the sink brushing her teeth. 'Hearing you talk, anyone would think you were living in a hovel with only animal hides for clothes. I don't want you to have this anxiety about money any more. You've become maddeningly materialistic.'

Rabih delivers his 'lesson' in such a frenzied manner (the doors are slammed very loudly indeed) not so much because he is a monster (though it would be unsurprising if a disinterested witness were, by this point, to reach such a conclusion) as because he is feeling both terrified and inadequate: terrified, because his wife and best friend in the world seems unable to comprehend a pivotal point about money and its relationship to fulfilment; and inadequate because he is incapable of providing Kirsten with what she now appears very much to want (fairly enough, he believes deep in his heart).

He badly needs his wife to see things from his point of view and yet has effectively lost any ability to help her do so.

We know that, when teaching students, only the utmost care and patience will ever work: we must never raise our voices, we have to use extraordinary tact, we must leave plenty of time for every lesson to sink in and we need to ensure at least ten compliments for every one delicately inserted negative remark. Above all, we must remain calm.

And yet the best guarantee of calm in a teacher is a relative indifference to the success or failure of his or her lesson. The serene teacher naturally wants things to go well, but if an obdurate pupil flunks, say, trigonometry, it is — at base — the pupil's problem. Tempers remain in check because individual students do not have very much power over their teachers' lives; they don't control their integrity and are not the chief determinants of their sense of contentment. An ability not to care too much is a critical aspect of unruffled and successful pedagogy.

But calm is precisely what is absent from love's classroom. There is simply too much on the line. The 'student' isn't merely a passing responsibility, he or she is a lifelong commitment. Failure will ruin existence. No wonder we may be prone to lose control and deliver cack-handed, hasty speeches which imply a lack of faith in the legitimacy or even the nobility of the act of imparting advice.

And no wonder, too, if we end up achieving the very opposite of our goals, because increasing levels of humiliation, anger and threat have seldom hastened anyone's development. Few of us ever grow more reasonable or more insightful about our own character for having had our self-esteem taken down a notch, our pride wounded and our ego subjected to a succession of pointed insults. We simply grow defensive and brittle in the face of suggestions which sound like mean-minded and senseless assaults on our nature, rather than caring attempts to address troublesome aspects of our personality.

Had Rabih picked up some better teaching habits, his lesson might have unfolded very differently. For a start, he would have made sure both of them went straight to bed and were well rested before anything was tackled. The next morning, he might have suggested a walk, perhaps to King George V Park, after they'd picked up a coffee and a pastry to have on a bench. Looking out at the large oak trees, he would have complimented Kirsten on the dinner and on a couple of other things, too, perhaps her skill at dealing with the politics in her office or her kindness to him over a package she'd posted for him the day before. Then, rather than accuse her, he would have implicated himself in the behaviour he wished to focus on. 'Teckle, I find myself getting so jealous of some of those types we know,' he would have started. 'If I hadn't gone into architecture, we could have had a summer villa, and I would have loved it in a lot of ways. I'm the first one to adore the sun and the Mediterranean. I dream of cool limestone floors and the smell of jasmine and thyme in the garden. I'm so sorry for letting us both down.' Then, like a doctor lulling the patient before jabbing the needle: 'What I also want to say, though, and it's probably a lesson for both of us, is that we're very lucky in a host of other ways that we should at least try not to forget. We're lucky that we have one another, that we enjoy our jobs on a good day, and that we know how to have a lot of fun on our rain-sodden summer holidays in the Outer Hebrides in a crofter's cottage that smells a little of sheep dung. For my part, so long as I'm with you, I'd quite frankly be happy living on this bench.'

But it isn't just Rabih who is a terrible teacher. Kirsten isn't a star student, either. Throughout their relationship, the two of them fail comprehensively at both tasks, teaching and learning. At the first sign that either one of them is adopting a pedagogical tone, the other assumes that they are under attack, which in turn causes them to close their ears to instruction and to react with sarcasm and aggression to suggestions, thereby generating further irritation and weariness in the mind of the fragile 'instructing' party.

'Rabih, no one has ever in my life said anything to me about my being *materialistic*,' responds Kirsten (in bed, ever more exhausted), deeply offended by the suggestion that she has noticed and envies her friends' lifestyles. 'In fact, only the other day, on the phone, Mum remarked that she'd never met anyone as modest and careful with money as me.'

'But that's slightly different, Teckle. We know she only says that because she loves you and you can do absolutely no wrong in her eyes.'

'You say that like it's a problem! Why can't you be just as blind if you love me?'

'Because I love you in a different way.'

'What way is that?'

'A way that makes me want to help you to confront certain issues.'

'A way that means you're going to be nasty!'

He knows his intentions have spun catastrophically out of control.

'I really do love you. I love you so much,' he says.

'So much that you're always wanting to change me? Rabih, I wish I understood . . .'

Harsh lessons allow pupils to fall back on the comforting thought that their instructor is simply crazy or nasty and that they themselves must therefore be, by logic, beyond criticism. Hearing an unreasonably extreme verdict can make us feel, consolingly, that our partner could not possibly be at once vicious and, in some small way, perhaps also right.

Sentimentally, we contrast the spousal negativity with the encouraging tone of our friends and family, on whom no remotely comparable set of demands has ever been made.

There are other ways to look at love. In their philosophy, the ancient Greeks offered a usefully unfashionable perspective on the relationship between love and teaching. In their eyes, love was first and foremost a feeling of admiration for the better sides of another human being. Love was the excitement of coming face to face with virtuous characteristics.

It followed that the deepening of love would always involve the desire to teach and in turn to be taught ways to become more virtuous: how to be less angry or less unforgiving, more curious or braver. Sincere lovers could never be content to accept one another just as they were; this would constitute a lazy and cowardly betrayal of the whole purpose of relationships. There would always be something to improve on in ourselves and educate others about.

Looked at through this ancient Greek lens, when lovers point out what might be unfortunate or uncomfortable about the other's character, they shouldn't be seen as giving up on the spirit of love. They should be congratulated for trying to do something very true to love's essence: helping their partners to develop into better versions of themselves.

In a more evolved world, one a little more alive to the Greek ideal of love, we would perhaps know to be a bit less clumsy, scared and aggressive when wanting to point something out, and rather less combative and sensitive when receiving feedback. The concept of education within a relationship would thus lose some of its unnecessarily eerie and negative connotations. We would accept that in responsible hands, both projects — teaching and being taught, calling attention to another's faults and letting ourselves be critiqued — might after all be loyal to the true purpose of love.

Rabih never does manage to control himself enough to get his point across. It will take a lot of time, and many more years of trying, before they properly master the art of teaching and learning.

But, in the meantime, Rabih's criticism of his wife on the materialistic score is blunted by one seismic humbling development. Five years into their marriage, at a highly auspicious moment in the property market, Kirsten manages to sell their flat, secure a new mortgage and acquire, at a very advantageous price, a light and comfortable house a few streets away, in Newbattle Terrace. The manoeuvre brings out all of her skills as a financial negotiator. Rabih observes her, up late at night checking different rates and up early sounding tough on the phone with estate agents, and concludes that he is exceptionally lucky to be married to a woman so obviously adept at dealing with money.

Along the way he also realizes something else. There may indeed be a side to Kirsten that is unusually alive to how others are doing financially and which aspires to a certain level of material comfort. This could be seen as a weakness, but in so far as it is one (and Rabih isn't even sure it is), it is intimately related to a strength. The price that Rabih must pay for relying on his wife's fiscal talent is having to endure certain associated downsides as well. The same virtues that make her a great negotiator and financial controller can also render her, sometimes – most particularly when he feels anxious about his career – a maddening and unsettling companion with whom to consider the achievements of others. In both scenarios, there is the same attachment to security, the same unwillingness to discount material criteria of success and the same intelligent concern for what things cost. Identical qualities produce both amazing house deals and insecurities around status. In her occasional worries about the relative wealth of her friends, Kirsten is – Rabih can now see – exhibiting nothing more or less than the weaknesses of her strengths.

Going forward, once they have moved into their new house, Rabih endeavours never to lose sight of those strengths, even at times when the weaknesses to which they can give rise are especially apparent.

CHILDREN

Love Lessons

Having always imagined that they would have children one day, they decide, four years into their marriage, to stop preventing the possibility. After seven months, they get the news beside the bathroom sink, in the form of a faint blue line within a cotton-backed porthole on a plastic stick – which doesn't seem a wholly fitting medium to herald the arrival of a new member of the race, a being who might still be around ninety-five years from now, and who will come to refer to the two presently underwear-clad people with an as yet unbelievable sobriquet: 'my parents'.

During the long months of the phoney war, they wonder what exactly they should be *doing*. Familiar with the difficulties of their own lives, they look on this as a chance to get everything right from the very start, beginning with the details. A Sunday supplement recommends more potato skins and raisins, herrings and walnut oil, which Kirsten zealously commits herself to as a way of warding off some of the terror she feels at her lack of control over everything occurring inside her. While she is in meetings or on the bus, at a party or doing the laundry, she knows that just a few millimetres from her bellybutton there are valves forming and neurons stitching, and DNA determining what sort of chin there will be, how the eyes will be set and which bits of their individual ancestries will make up the filaments of a personality. Small wonder she goes to bed early. She has never been so concerned about anything in her life.

Rabih often places his hand protectively over her belly. What's going on inside is so much cleverer than they are. Together, they know how to do budgets, calculate traffic projections, design floor plans; what's inside knows how to build itself a skull and a pump that will function for almost a century without resting for so much as a single beat.

In the last weeks, they envy the alien its final moments of complete unity and understanding. They imagine that in later life, perhaps in some foreign hotel room, after a long flight, it will try to drown out the noise from the air conditioning and dampen the disorientation of jet lag by curling up into itself in that original foetal position in search of the primordial peace of the long-lost maternal brine.

When she at last emerges after a seven-hour ordeal, they call her Esther, after one of her maternal great-grandmothers, and Katrin, after Rabih's mother. They can't stop looking at her. She appears perfect in every way, the most beautiful creature they have ever seen, staring at both of them with enormous eyes that seem infinitely wise – as if she had spent a previous life absorbing every volume of wisdom in the world. That wide forehead, those finely crafted fingers and those feet as soft as eyelids will later, during the long sleepless nights, play a not-incidental role in calming nerves when the wailing threatens to test parental sanity.

At once they begin to fret about the planet they have brought her into. The hospital walls are a sickly green; she is held awkwardly by a nurse and jabbed at by a doctor's enquiring spatula; screaming and banging can be heard from neighbouring wards; she's alternately too hot and too cold – and in the exhaustion and chaos of the early hours, there seems little else left for her but to weep without measure. The cries pierce the hearts of her desperate attendants, who can find no dictionary with which to translate her furious commands. Huge hands stroke her head and voices keep murmuring things she can't make sense of. The overhead lamps emit a fierce white light, which her paper-thin eyelids are not yet strong enough to resist. The task of latching on to the nipple is like trying to cling for life to a buoy amid a raging ocean storm. She is, to put it mildly, a bit out of sorts. After titanic struggles, she eventually falls asleep on the outside of her old home, heartbroken to have left without keys, but comforted somewhat by the rise and fall of familiar breaths.

Never have they cared so intensely and comprehensively about anyone. Her arrival transforms what they understand about love. They recognize how little they had previously grasped of what might be at stake.

Maturity means acknowledging that Romantic love might constitute only a narrow, and perhaps rather mean-minded, aspect of emotional life, one principally focused on a quest to find love rather than to give it; to be loved rather than to love.

Children may end up being the unexpected teachers of people many times their age, to whom they offer — through their exhaustive depend-ence, egoism and vulnerability — an advanced education in a wholly new sort of love, one in which reciprocation is never jealously demanded or fractiously regretted and in which the true goal is nothing less than the transcendence of oneself for the sake of another.

The morning after the birth, the nurses discharge the new family without guidance or advice, save for one leaflet about colic and another about immunizations. The average home appliance comes with more detailed instructions than a baby, society maintaining a touching belief that there is nothing much that one generation can, in the end, reasonably tell another about life.

Children teach us that love is, in its purest form, a kind of service. The word has grown freighted with negative connotations. An individualistic, self-gratifying culture cannot easily equate contentment with being at someone else's call. We are used to loving others in return for what they can do for us, for their capacity to entertain, charm or soothe us. Yet babies can do precisely nothing. There is, as slightly older children sometimes conclude with a sense of serious discomfort, no 'point' to them; that is their point. They teach us to give without expecting anything in return, simply because they need help badly – and we are in a position to provide it. We are inducted into a love based not on an admiration for strength, but on a compassion for weakness, a vulnerability common to every member of the species and one which has been and will eventually again be our own. Because it is always tempting to overemphasize autonomy and independence, these helpless creatures are here to remind us that no one is, in the end, 'self-made'; we are all heavily in someone's debt. We realize that life depends – quite literally – on the capacity for love.

We learn, too, that being another's servant is not humiliating, quite the opposite, for it sets us free from the wearying responsibility of continuously catering to our own twisted, insatiable natures. We learn the relief and privilege of being granted something more important to live for than ourselves.

They wipe her little bottom, time and time again – and wonder why they never really understood clearly before that this really is what one human has to do for another. They warm bottles for her in the middle of the night, they are overwhelmed with relief if she sleeps for more than an hour at a stretch, they worry about, and argue over, the timing of her burps. All of this she will later forget and they will be unable or unwilling to convey to her. Gratitude will come to them only indirectly, through the knowledge that she herself will, one day, have a sufficient sense of inner well-being to want to do this for somebody else.

Her sheer incompetence is awe-inspiring. Everything must be learned: how to curl fingers around a cup, how to swallow a piece of banana, how to move a hand across the rug to grasp a key. Nothing comes easily. A morning's work might include stacking up bricks and knocking them down, banging a fork against the table, dropping stones into a puddle, pulling a book about Hindu temple architecture off a shelf, seeing what Mama's finger might taste like. Everything is amazing – once.

Neither Kirsten nor Rabih has ever known such a mixture of love and boredom. They are used to basing their friendships on shared temperaments and interests. But Esther is, confusingly, simultaneously the most boring person they have ever met and the one they find themselves loving the most. Rarely have love and psychological compatibility drifted so far apart – and yet it doesn't matter in the slightest. Perhaps all that emphasis on having 'something in common' with others is overdone: Rabih and Kirsten have a new sense of how little is in truth required to form a bond with another human being. Anyone who urgently needs us deserves, in the true book of love, to be our friend.

Literature has seldom dwelt long in the playroom and the nursery, and perhaps for good reason. In older novels, wet nurses swiftly bear infants away, so that the action can resume. In the living room in Newbattle Terrace, for months, nothing much happens in the outward sense. The hours appear to be empty, but in truth everything is in them. Esther will forget their details entirely when she finally awakens as a coherent consciousness from the long night of early childhood. But their enduring legacy will be a primary sense of ease with and trust in the world. The fundamentals of Esther's childhood will be stored not so much in events as in sensory memories: of being held close to someone's chest, of certain slants of light at particular times of day, of smells, types of biscuits, textures of carpet, the distant, incomprehensible, soothing sound of her parents' voices in the car during long night-time drives and an underlying feeling that she has a right to exist and reasons to go on hoping.

The child teaches the adult something else about love: that genuine love should involve a constant attempt to interpret with maximal generosity what might be going on, at any time, beneath the surface of difficult and unappealing behaviour.

The parent has to second-guess what the cry, the kick, the grief or the anger is really about. And what marks out this project of interpretation — and makes it so different from what occurs in the average adult relationship — is its charity. Parents are apt to proceed from the assumption that their children, though they may be troubled or in pain, are fundamentally good. As soon as the particular pin that is jabbing them is correctly identified, they will be restored to native innocence. When children cry, we don't accuse them of being mean or self-pitying; we wonder what has upset them. When they bite, we know they must be frightened or momentarily vexed. We are alive to the insidious effects that hunger, a tricky digestive tract or a lack of sleep may have on mood.

How kind we would be if we managed to import even a little of this instinct into adult relationships — if here, too, we could look past the grumpiness and viciousness and recognize the fear, confusion and exhaustion which almost invariably underlie them. This is what it would mean to gaze upon the human race with love.

Esther's first Christmas is spent with her grandmother. She cries for most of the train journey up to Inverness. Her mother and father are pale and wrung out by the time they reach her grandmother's terraced house. Something is hurting Esther inside, but she has no way of knowing what or where. The attendants' hunch is that she is too hot. A blanket is removed, then tucked around her again. New ideas come to mind: it might be thirst, or perhaps the sun, or the noise from the television, or the soap they have been using or an allergy to her sheets. Most tellingly, it isn't ever assumed to be mere petulance or sourness; the child is only ever, deep down, good.

The attendants simply cannot get to the root cause, despite trying milk, a back rub, talcum powder, caresses, a less itchy collar, sitting up, lying down, a bath and a walk up and down the stairs. In the end, the poor creature vomits an alarming confection of banana and brown rice across her new linen dress, her first Christmas present, on which her grandmother has embroidered 'Esther', and falls asleep at once. Not for the last time, but with infinitely greater concern from those around her, she is violently misunderstood.

As parents, we learn another thing about love: how much power we have over people who depend on us and, therefore, what responsibilities we have to tread carefully around those who have been placed at our mercy. We learn of an unexpected power to hurt without meaning to: to frighten through eccentricity or unpredictability, anxiety or momentary irritation. We must train ourselves, to be as others need us to be rather than as our own first reflexes might dictate. The barbarian must will himself to hold the crystal goblet lightly, in a meaty fist that could otherwise crush it like a dry autumn leaf.

Rabih likes to play at being various animals when he looks after Esther in the early morning at weekends, when Kirsten is catching up on sleep. It takes Rabih a while to appreciate how scary he can appear. It has never occurred to him before what a giant he is, how peculiar and threatening his eyes might look, how aggressive his voice can sound. The pretend lion, on all fours on the carpet, finds to his horror that his little playmate is screaming for help and refuses to be calmed down, despite his assurances that the nasty old lion has now gone away and Dada is back. She wants no part of him; only the gentler, more careful Mama (who has to be roused from bed in an emergency and is not especially grateful to Rabih as a result) will do.

He recognizes how cautious he has to be when introducing aspects of the world to her. There cannot be ghosts; the very word has the power to inspire terror. Nor does one joke about dragons, especially after dark. It matters how he first describes the police to her, and the different political parties and Christian–Muslim relations . . . He realizes that he will never know anyone in such an unguarded state as he has been able to know her – having witnessed her struggling heroically to roll from her back on to her stomach and to write her first word – and that it must be his solemn duty never to use her weakness against her.

Although cynical by nature, he is now utterly on the side of hope in presenting the world to her. Thus the politicians are trying their best; scientists are right now working on curing diseases; and this would be a very good time to turn off the radio. In some of the more run-down neighbourhoods they drive through, he feels like an apologetic official giving a tour to a foreign dignitary. The graffiti will soon be cleaned up, those hooded figures are shouting because they're happy, the trees are beautiful at this time of year . . . In the company of his small passenger, he is reliably ashamed of his fellow adults.

As for his own nature, it too has been sanitized and simplified.

At home he is 'Dada', a man untroubled by career or financial worries, a lover of ice cream, a goofy figure who likes nothing more than to spin his wee girl around and lift her on to his shoulders. He loves Esther far too much to dare impose his anxious reality upon her. Loving her means striving to have the courage not to be entirely himself.

The world thereby assumes, during Esther's early years, a kind of stability that she will later feel it must subsequently have lost – but which in fact it only ever had thanks to her parents' determined and judicious editing. Its solidity and sense of longevity are an illusion believable only to one who doesn't yet understand how haphazard life can be, and how constant are change and destruction. To her, for example, the house in Newbattle Terrace is simply and naturally 'home', with all the eternal associations of that word, rather than a quite ordinary house picked according to expedient considerations. The degree of repressed contingency reaches its apogee in the case of Esther's own existence. Had Kirsten's and Rabih's lives unfolded only slightly differently, the constellation of physical features and character traits which now seem so indelibly and necessarily coalesced under their daughter's name might have belonged to other entities altogether, hypothetical people who would forever remain frozen as unrealized possibilities, scattered genetic potential that never got used because someone cancelled dinner, already had a boyfriend or was too shy to ask for a phone number.

The carpet in Esther's room, a beige woollen expanse on which she spends hours cutting out pieces of paper in the shapes of animals and from which she looks up at the sky through her window on sunny afternoons, will have for her the immemorial feel of the surface on which she first learned to crawl, and whose distinctive smell and texture she'll remember for the rest of her days. But for her parents, it was hardly predestined to be an impregnable totem of domestic identity: it was in fact ordered just a few weeks before Esther's birth, in something of a hurry, from an unreliable local salesman on the high street next to the bus stop who went out of business shortly thereafter. Part of the reassuring aspect of being new to the earth stems from the failure to understand the tenuous nature of everything.

A well-loved child is set a challenging precedent. By its very nature, parental love works to conceal the effort which went into generating it. It shields the recipient from the donor's complexity and sadness — and from an awareness of how many other interests, friends and concerns the parent has sacrificed in the name of love. With infinite generosity, it places the small person at the very centre of the cosmos for a time — to give it strength for the day he or she will, with agonizing surprise, have to grasp the true scale, and awkward solitude, of the grown-up world.

On a typical evening in Edinburgh, when Rabih and Kirsten have finally settled Esther, when her well-ironed cloth is by her chin, she is snug in her baby-grow, and all is quiet on the baby monitor in the bedroom, these two infinitely patient and kind carers retreat to their quarters, reach for the TV or the leftover Sunday magazines and swiftly lapse into a pattern of behaviour which might rather shock the child, were she miraculously capable of observing and comprehending the interactions. For in the place of the soft, indulgent language Rabih and Kirsten have been using with their child for many hours, there is often just bitterness, vengeance and carping. The effort of love has exhausted them. They have nothing left to give to one another. The tired child inside each of them is furious at how long it has been neglected and is in pieces.

It isn't surprising if, as adults, when we first start to form relationships, we should devotedly go off in search of someone who can give us the all-encompassing, selfless love that we may once have known in childhood. Nor would it be surprising if we were to feel frustrated and in the end extremely bitter at how difficult it seems to be to find; at how seldom people know how to help us as they should. We may rage and blame others for their inability to intuit our needs, we may fitfully move from one relationship to another, we may blame an entire sex for its shallowness — until the day we end our quixotic searches and reach a semblance of mature detachment, realizing that the only release from our longing may be to stop demanding a perfect love and noting its many absences at every turn, and instead start to give love away (perhaps to a small person) with oblivious abandon without jealously calculating the chances of it ever returning.

Sweetness

Three years after Esther's arrival, William is born. He has a cheeky, winsome nature from the first. His parents will always remain convinced that only a few hours after leaving the womb, with apparent knowingness, he winked at them from his crib. By the time he's four, there will be few hearts he leaves entirely cold. There is sweetness in the questions he asks, the games he plays and the repeated offers he makes to marry his sister.

Childhood sweetness: the immature part of goodness, as seen through the prism of adult experience, which is to say from the far side of a substantial amount of suffering, renunciation and discipline.

We label as 'sweet' children's open displays of hope, trust, spontaneity, wonder and simplicity — qualities which are under severe threat, but are deeply longed for in the ordinary run of grown-up life. The sweetness of children reminds us of how much we have had to sacrifice on the path to maturity; the sweet is a vital part of ourselves — in exile.

Rabih misses his children with particular intensity when he's at work. In a setting marked by constant tension and professional manoeuvring, the very idea of their trust and vulnerability seems poignant. He finds it almost heartbreaking to remember that there is a place not far away from his office where people know how to care properly about one another, and where a person's tears and confusion, let alone lunch menu and sleeping position, can be of such deep concern to another human.

It can't be coincidental that the sweetness of children should be especially easy to identify and cherish at this point in history. Societies become sensitive to the qualities they are missing. A world that demands high degrees of self-control, cynicism and rationality, and is marked by extreme insecurity and competitiveness, justly sees in childhood its own counterbalancing virtues, qualities that have too sternly and definitively had to be surrendered in return for the keys to the adult realm.

William is pleased by a panoply of things that the grown-ups around him have forgotten to marvel at: ants' nests, balloons, juicy colouring pens, snails, ear wax, the roar of a plane at take-off, going underwater in the bath . . . He is an enthusiast of a class of uncomplicated things which have – unfairly – become boring to adults; like a great artist, he is master at renewing his audience's appreciation of the so-called minor sides of life.

He is a particular fan, for instance, of 'bed-jumping'. You've got to have a long runway, he explains, it's best if you can start out in the corridor with the bed covered in a huge pile of pillows and the sofa cushions from downstairs. It's crucial that you get your arms properly up in the air as you run towards the target. When older people like Mama and Dada have a go, they tend to hold back and keep their arms down by their sides, or else they do that half-hearted thing where they kind of clench their fists and keep them up near their chest. Either one reduces the pay-off quite a lot.

Then there are the many important questions that need to be asked throughout the day: 'Why is there dust?', 'If you shaved a baby gorilla, would it look like a human baby?', 'When will I stop being a child?' Anything can be a good starting point for curiosity, when you haven't yet got to the stifling stage of supposedly knowing where your interests lie.

He's not worried about seeming abnormal, for there is as yet, blessedly, no such category in his imagination. His emotions remain unguarded. He is not afraid – for now – of humiliation. He doesn't know about notions of respectability, cleverness or manliness, those catastrophic inhibitors of talent and spirit. His early childhood is like a laboratory for what humanity in general might be like if there were no such thing as ridicule.

Sometimes, when the mood strikes, he likes to wear his mother's heels and her bra and wants to be addressed as Lady William. He admires the hair of his classmate Arjun and tells Kirsten with considerable excitement one evening just how much he'd like to stroke it. Arjun would be a very nice husband to have, he adds.

His drawings add to the sweetness. Partly it's their exuberant optimism. The sun is always out, people are smiling. There's no attempt to peer below the surface and discover compromises and evasions. In his parents' eyes, there's nothing trivial whatsoever about such cheer: hope is an achievement and their little boy is a champion at it. There's charm in his utter indifference to getting scenes 'right'. Later, when art classes begin at school, he will be taught the rules of drawing and advised to pay precise attention to what is before his eyes. But for now, he doesn't have to concern himself with how exactly a branch is attached to a tree trunk or what people's legs and hands look like. He is gleefully unconcerned with the true and often dull facts of the universe. He cares only about what he feels and what seems like fun at this precise moment; he reminds his parents that there can be a good side to uninhibited egoism.

Even William's and Esther's fears are sweet, because they are so easy to calm, and so unrelated to what there is truly to be frightened of in the world. They're about wolves and monsters, malaria and sharks. The children are, of course, correct to be scared; they just don't have the right targets in mind — yet. They aren't informed about the real horrors waiting for them in adulthood: exploitation, deceit, career disaster, envy, abandonment and mortality. The children's anxieties are unconscious apprehensions of the true midlife terrors, except that when these finally have to be confronted, the world won't find their owners quite so endearing or such fitting targets for reassurance and a cuddle.

Esther regularly comes into Rabih and Kirsten's bedroom at around two a.m., carrying Dobbie with her and complaining of some bad dreams about a dragon. She lies between them, one hand allotted to each parent, her thin legs touching theirs. Her helplessness makes them feel strong. The comfort she needs is entirely within their power to provide. They will kill the daft dragon if he dares to turn up around here.

They watch her fall back to sleep, her eyelids trembling a little, Dobbie tucked in next to her. They stay awake a while, moved, because they know their little girl will have to grow up, leave them, suffer, be rejected and have her heart broken. She will be out in the world, will long for reassurance but will be out of their reach. There will, eventually, be some real dragons, and Mama and Dada will be quite unable to dispatch them.

It's not just children who are childlike. Adults, too, are — beneath the bluster — intermittently playful, silly, fanciful, vulnerable, hysterical, terrified, pitiful and in search of consolation and forgiveness.

We're well versed at seeing the sweet and the fragile in children and offering them help and comfort accordingly. Around them, we know how to put aside the worst of our compulsions, vindictiveness and fury. We can recalibrate our expectations and demand a little less than we normally do; we're slower to anger and a bit more aware of unrealized potential. We readily treat children with a degree of kindness that we are oddly and woefully reluctant to show to our peers.

It is a wonderful thing to live in a world where so many people are nice to children. It would be even better if we lived in one where we were a little nicer to the childlike sides of one another.

The Limits of Love

Rabih and Kirsten's first priority with Esther and William – it is ranked infinitely higher than any other – is to be kind, because everywhere around them they see examples of what happens, they believe, when love is in short supply: breakdowns and resentments, shame and addiction, chronic failures of self-confidence and inabilities to form sound relationships. In Rabih and Kirsten's eyes, when there is insufficient nurture, when parents are remote and domineering, unreliable and frightening, life can never feel complete. No one can hope to be strong enough to negotiate the thick tangles of existence, they maintain, without having once enjoyed a sense of mattering limitlessly and inordinately to one or two adults.

This is why they strive to answer every question with tenderness and sensitivity, punctuate the days with cuddles, read long stories in the evenings, get up to play at dawn, go easy on the children when they make mistakes, forgive their naughty moments and allow their toys to remain strewn across the living-room carpet overnight.

Their faith in the power of parental kindness reaches a pitch in Esther's and William's earliest years, particularly at those moments when they are finally asleep in their cots, defenceless before the world, their breath coming light and steady and their finely formed fingers clenched around their favourite blankets.

But by the time each of them turns five, a more complicated and troubling reality comes into view: Rabih and Kirsten are, to their surprise, brought up against certain stubborn limits of kindness.

One rainy weekend in February, Rabih buys William an orange remote-controlled helicopter. Father and son spotted it on the internet a few weeks before, and since then they have talked to each other of little else. Eventually Rabih caved in, even though there's no impending birthday or gratifying school mark to justify the gift. Still, it will surely provide them with hours of fun. But after only six minutes' use, as the toy is hovering over the dining table with Rabih at the controls, something goes wrong with the steering, the machine collides with the fridge and the back rotor snaps into pieces. The fault lies squarely with the manufacturers, but sadly they are not present in the kitchen – so, at once and not for the first time, it is Rabih who becomes the target of his child's acute disappointment.

'What have you done?' shrieks William, whose sweetness is now very much in abeyance.

'Nothing,' replies Rabih. 'The thing just went berserk.'

'It didn't. You did something. You have to fix it now.'

'Of course I'd love to do that. But it's complicated. We'll have to get in touch with the shop on Monday.'

'Dada!' This comes out as a scream.

'Darling, I know you must be disappointed, but –'

'It's your fault!'

Tears start to flow, and a moment later William attempts to kick the incompetent pilot in the shins. The boy's behaviour is appalling, of course, and a little surprising (Dada meant so well!), but on this occasion, as on more than a few others, it also stands as a perverse sort of tribute to Rabih as a father. A person has to feel rather safe around someone else in order to be this difficult. Before a child can throw a tantrum, the background atmosphere needs to be profoundly benevolent. Rabih himself wasn't anything like this tricky with his own father when he was young, but then again, neither did he ever feel quite so loved by him. All the assurances he and Kirsten have offered over the years – 'I will always be on your side', 'You can tell us whatever you're feeling' – have paid off brilliantly: they have encouraged William and his sister to direct their frustrations and disappointments powerfully towards the two loving adults who have signalled that they can, and will, take the heat.

Witnessing their children's rages, Rabih and Kirsten have a chance to note how much restraint and patience they themselves have, without fully realizing it, developed over the years. Their somewhat more equable temperaments are the legacy of decades of minor and more major disappointments; the patient courses of their thought processes have been carved out, like canyons by the flow of water, by all the many things that have gone wrong for them. Rabih doesn't throw a tantrum when he makes a stray mark on a sheet of paper he's writing on because, among other things, he has in the past lost his job and seen his mother die.

The role of being a good parent brings with it one large and very tricky requirement: to be the constant bearer of deeply unfortunate news. The good parent must be the defender of a range of the child's long-term interests, which are by nature entirely impossible for him or her to envisage, let alone assent to cheerfully. Out of love, parents must gird themselves to speak of clean teeth, homework, tidy rooms, bedtimes, generosity and limits to computer usage. Out of love, they must adopt the guise of bores with a hateful and maddening habit of bringing up unwelcome facts about existence just when the fun is really starting.

And, as a result of these subterranean loving acts, good parents must, if things have gone well, end up as the special targets of intense resentment and indignation.

However difficult the messages may be, Rabih and Kirsten begin with a commitment to imparting them gently: 'Just five more minutes of playtime and then the game is over, OK?', 'Time for Princess E's bath now', 'That must have been annoying for you, but we don't hit people who disagree with us, remember?'

They want to coax and wheedle and, most importantly, never impose a conclusion through force or the use of basic psychological weapons, such as reminders about who is the older, bigger and wealthier party and is, ergo, in charge of the remote control and the laptop.

'Because I am your mother', 'Because your father said so': there was a time when these relational titles alone commanded obedience. But the meaning of the words has been transformed by our era of kindness, so that a mother and father are now merely 'people who will make it nice for me' or 'people whose suggestions I may go along with if – and only if – I see the point of what they're saying'.

Unhappily, there are situations in which coaxing won't work any more – for example, on the occasion when Esther starts to tease William about his body, and a gentle maternal caution goes unheard. His penis is an 'ugly sausage', Esther yells repeatedly at home, and then, even less kindly, she whispers the same metaphor to a band of her girlfriends at school.

Her parents try tactfully to explain that her taunting him now, to the point of humiliation, might make it harder for him to relate to women when he gets older. But this of course sounds weird to his sister. She replies that they don't understand anything, that William really has got an ugly sausage between his legs and that this is why everyone is laughing at school.

It isn't their daughter's fault that, at nine years old, she can't begin to appreciate the nature of her parents' alarm (and, offstage, a little laughter too). But it's still galling when Esther, having been told firmly to stop it, accuses them of interfering in her life and writes the words *Fun Spoilers* on little pieces of paper that she leaves like a trail of breadcrumbs around the house.

The dispute ends in a shouting match between Rabih and this incensed small person who is, somewhere in her brain, simply lacking in the particular neuronal connections which would allow her to grasp what is at stake here.

'Because I say so,' says Rabih. 'Because you are nine and I am considerably older and know a few things you don't – and I'm not going to stand here all day and have an argument with you about it.'

'That's so unfair! Then I'm just going to shout and shout,' threatens Esther.

'You'll do no such thing, young lady. You'll go up to your room and stay there until you're ready to come down again and rejoin the family for dinner and behave in a civilized way and show me you've got some manners.'

It's a strange thing indeed for Rabih, congenitally intent as he is on avoiding confrontation of any sort, to have to deliver such an apparently unloving message to someone he loves beyond measure.

The dream is to save the child time; to pass on in one go insights that required arduous and lengthy experience to accumulate. But the progress of the human race is at every turn stymied by an ingrained resistance to being rushed to conclusions. We are held back by an inherent interest in re-exploring entire chapters in the back catalogue of our species' idiocies — and to wasting a good part of life finding out for ourselves what has already been extensively and painfully charted by others.

Romanticism has traditionally been suspicious of rules in child-rearing, regarding them as a fake hypocritical bunting unnecessarily draped over children's endearing natural goodness. However, after closer acquaintance with a few flesh-and-blood youngsters, we might gradually change our mind and come to the view that manners are in truth an incontrovertible defence against an ever-present danger of something close to barbarism. Manners don't have to be an instrument of coldness and sadism, just a way of teaching us to keep the beast-like bit locked up inside, so that the evening meal does not invariably have to descend into anarchy.

Rabih wonders sometimes where all the immensely hard parental work is really leading them – what the hours they have spent picking up the children from school, talking to them and coaxing and reasoning with them, have been for. He began by hoping, naively and selfishly, that he and Kirsten were raising better versions of themselves. It's taken him a while to realize that he has instead helped to put on earth two people with an inbuilt mission to challenge him, individuals who will inflict upon him repeated frustrations, frequent bewilderment and a forced, unsettling and occasionally beautiful expansion of his interests far beyond anything he could ever have imagined, into hitherto alien realms of ice skating, TV sitcoms, pink dresses, space exploration and the standing of Hearts in the Scottish Premiership.

At the children's school, a well-meaning small establishment nearby, watching from some remove as the other parents drop off their precious charges, Rabih reflects that life can never reward on a large enough scale all the hopes which one generation places on the narrow shoulders of another. There aren't sufficient glorious destinies to hand, and the traps are too many and too easy to fall into, even if a golden star and an ovation may be in the offing for a well-delivered reading, in assembly, of a poem about ravens.

At times the protective veil of paternal sentimentality slips and Rabih sees that he has given over a very substantial share of the best days of his life to a pair of human beings who, if they weren't his own children, would almost surely strike him as being fundamentally unremarkable – so much so, in fact, that were he to meet them in a pub in thirty years' time, he might prefer not even to talk to them. The insight is unendurable.

Whatever modest denials parents may offer, however much they may downplay their ambitions in front of strangers, to have a child is – at the outset, at least – to make an assault on perfection, to attempt to create not just another average human being but an exemplar of distinctive perfection. Mediocrity, albeit the statistical norm, can never be the initial goal; the sacrifices required to get a child to adulthood are simply too great.

It's a Saturday afternoon and William is out playing football with a friend. Esther has stayed at home to put together the electronic circuit board she got for her birthday a few months back. She has enlisted Rabih's help, and together they're going through the instruction manual, wiring up bulbs and little motors and delighting in those moments when the whole system whirrs into action. Rabih likes to tell his daughter that she would make a great electrical engineer. He can't quite let go of his fantasy of her as an adult woman who will somehow manage to be at once entirely practical and yet also lyrically sensitive (a version of every woman he has loved). Esther adores the attention. She looks forward to the rare occasions when William is away and she has her dad all to herself. He calls her Besti; she sits on his lap and, when he hasn't shaved for a day, complains about how strange and rough his skin feels. He brushes her hair back and covers her forehead with kisses. Kirsten watches them from across the room. Once, when Esther was four, she said to both her parents, with great seriousness, 'I wish Mummy would die so I could marry Daddy.' Kirsten understands. She herself might have liked to have a kind and reliable father to cuddle and build circuits with, and no one else around to bother them. She can see what a bewitching and glamorous figure Rabih could seem to someone under ten. He's happy to get on the floor and play with Esther's dolls, he takes her rock climbing, buys her dresses, goes cycling with her and talks to her about the brilliant engineers who built Scotland's tunnels and bridges.

The relationship nevertheless makes Kirsten worry a little for her daughter's future. She wonders how other men will be able to measure up to such standards of tenderness and focused attention – and whether Besti may end up rejecting a range of candidates based on nothing more than the fact that they don't come close to offering her the sort of friendship she once enjoyed with her dad. Yet what niggles Kirsten most of all is the sentimentality of Rabih's performance. She knows at first hand that the kindness he displays with their daughter is available from him only in his role as a father, not as a husband. She has plenty of experience with his drastic change in tone once the two of them are out of earshot of the children. He is unwittingly planting an image in Esther's mind of how a man might ideally behave with a woman – notwithstanding that the ideal in no way reflects the truth of who he, Rabih, really is. Thus Esther may, in later life, ask a man who is acting in a selfish, distracted and severe manner why he can't be more like her father, little realizing that he is actually remarkably like Rabih, just not the version of him that she ever got to see.

In the circumstances, it's perhaps helpful that kindness has its limits and that these two parents, despite their best efforts, still manage (like all parents) regularly and deeply to annoy their children. Being downright cold, frightening and cruel turns out to be only the first of many different means of ensuring alienation. Another quite effective strategy combines overprotectiveness, over-involvement and over-cuddling, a trio of neurotic behaviours with which Rabih and Kirsten are deeply familiar. Rabih, the Beirut boy, frets about Esther and William every time they cross a road; he seeks a potentially vexing degree of closeness to them, asks them too often how their day was, always wants them to put on another layer of clothing and imagines them as being more fragile than they really are – which is partly why Esther more than once snaps, 'Get off my case!' at him, and not without cause.

Nor, indeed, can it be all that easy to have Kirsten as their mother, for this entails having to do a lot of extra spelling tests, being encouraged to play several musical instruments and hearing continual reminders to eat healthy foods – a not entirely surprising set of priorities from someone who was the only student in her secondary-school class to go to university, and one of a minority not now living on benefits.

In certain moods Rabih can pity the children for having to deal with the two of them. He can understand their complaints about and resentment of the power that he and Kirsten wield over them, their thirty-plus-year head start and the droning sound of their voices in the kitchen every morning. He has sufficient trouble coping with himself so it isn't too much of a leap for him to sympathize with two young people who may have one or two issues with him. Their irritation, he also knows, has its own important role to play: it's what guarantees that the children will one day leave home.

If parental kindness were enough, the human race would stagnate and in time die off. The survival of the species hinges on children eventually getting fed up and heading off into the world, armed with hopes of finding more satisfying sources of love and excitement.

In their moments of cosiness, when the whole family is piled together on the big bed and the mood is one of tolerance and good humour, Rabih is aware that some day, in the not too distant future, all of this will end, according to an edict of nature enacted by a most natural means: the tantrums and fury of adolescence. The continuation of families down the generations depends on the young ones eventually losing patience with their elders. It would be a tragedy if the four of them still wanted to lie here with their limbs enlaced in another twenty-five years' time. Esther and William will ultimately have to begin finding him and Kirsten ridiculous, boring and old-fashioned, in order to develop the impetus to move out of the house.

Their daughter has recently assumed a leadership role in the resistance to parental rule. As she approaches her eleventh birthday, she starts to take exception to her father's clothes, his accent and his way of cooking, and rolls her eyes at her mother's concern with reading good literature and her absurd habit of keeping lemon halves in the fridge rather than more carelessly tossing the unused bit away. The taller and stronger Esther grows, the more she is irritated by her parents' behaviour and habits. William is still too little to cast such a caustic eye at his carers. Nature is gentle with children in this regard, making them sensitive to the full array of their forebears' flaws only at an age when they are big enough to flee them.

In order to let the separation take its course, Rabih and Kirsten know not to become too strict, distant or intimidating. They understand how easy it is for children to get hung up on a mum or dad who is hard to read, scary-seeming or just not around all that much. Such parents can hook in their offspring more tightly than the responsive and stable ones will ever do. Rabih and Kirsten have no wish to be the sort of self-centred, volatile figures with whom a child can become obsessed for life, and so take care to be natural, approachable and even, sometimes, theatrically daft. They want to be unintimidating enough that Esther and William will be able, when the time comes, to park them cleanly to one side and get on with their lives. Being taken a bit for granted is, they implicitly feel, the best possible indication of the quality of their love.

Sex and Parenthood

'Let's do it tonight. What do you think?' says Kirsten, as she puts on her make-up in the bathroom before heading downstairs to prepare the children's breakfast.

'You're on,' says Rabih, with a smile, adding, 'I'll put it in my diary now.' He's not joking. Friday night is a favoured slot and it's been a while.

On his way to work, he thinks of Kirsten's dark wet hair, which beautifully offset her pale skin when she stepped out of the shower. He takes a moment to appreciate his extraordinary good fortune that this elegant, determined Scottish woman has agreed to spend her life beside him.

The day turns out to be rather stressful and it's not till seven that he reaches home again. He's longing for Kirsten now, but he has to be diplomatic. There can be no rush and certainly no demands. He is going to try to tell her with particular honesty what he feels beneath the everyday turbulence. The plan is hazy, but he is hopeful.

The family are all in the kitchen, where there's a tense discussion unfolding about fruit. Both of the children are flatly refusing to have any, despite Kirsten's having been out to buy some blueberries especially and laying them out on a plate in the shape of a smiling face. William accuses his mother of being mean, Esther wails that the smell of the fruit is making her ill.

Rabih attempts a joke about having missed being in the asylum, ruffles William's hair and suggests it might be time for stories upstairs. Rabih and Kirsten alternate reading to them in the evenings and tonight it's her turn. In their room, she pulls them close to her, one on each side, and begins a story, translated from the German, about a rabbit pursued by hunters in a forest. Seeing them huddled against her reminds Rabih of how it used to be with his own mother. William likes to play with Kirsten's hair, pushing it right forward, just as Rabih used to do. When the story is over, they want more, so she sings them an old Scottish lullaby, 'Griogal Cridhe', which tells the tragic tale of a young widow whose husband was taken prisoner and executed in front of her by her own clan. He sits on the landing, moved, listening to Kirsten's voice. He feels privileged to have witnessed his wife's evolution into an exceptionally competent mother. She, at this point, would above all love a beer.

Rabih goes to lie down on their bed. Half an hour later, he hears Kirsten enter the bathroom. When she emerges, it is in the tartan dressing gown that she has had since she was fifteen and which she used to wear a lot when the children were very small. He is starting to wonder how he might begin when she mentions a phone call she had that afternoon with a friend in the United States whom she knew as a student at Aberdeen. The poor woman's mother has been diagnosed with oesophageal cancer, the verdict came out of the blue. Not for the first time, he senses what a good friend Kirsten is, and how deeply and instinctively she enters into the needs of others.

Then Kirsten mentions that she has been thinking about the children's university education. It is a long way off still, but that's exactly the point. Now is the time to start putting something aside, not much – they are squeezed – but enough to build into a useful sum eventually.

Rabih clears his throat and, somewhere inside, becomes a little desperate.

We might imagine that the fear and insecurity of getting close to someone would happen only once: at the start of a relationship, and that anxieties couldn't possibly continue after two people had made some explicit commitments to one another, like marrying, securing a joint mortgage, buying a house, having a few children and naming each other in their wills.

Yet conquering distance and gaining assurances that we are needed aren't exercises to be performed only once; they have to be repeated every time there's been a break – a day away, a busy period, an evening at work – for every interlude has the power once again to raise the question of whether or not we are still wanted.

It's therefore a pity how hard it is to find a stigma-free and winning way of admitting to the intensity of our need for reassurance. Even after years together, there remains a hurdle of fear around asking for a proof of desire. But with a horrible, added complication: we now assume that any such anxiety couldn't legitimately exist. Hence the temptation to pretend that reassurance would be the last thing on our minds. We might even, strangely, have an affair, an act of betrayal that is all too often simply a face-saving attempt to pretend we don't need someone, an arduous proof of indifference that we reserve for, and secretly address to, the person we truly care about but are terrified of showing that we need and have been inadvertently hurt by.

We are never through with the requirement for acceptance. This isn't a curse limited to the inadequate and the weak. Insecurity may even be a peculiar sign of well-being. It means we haven't allowed ourselves to take

other people for granted, that we remain realistic enough to see that things
could genuinely turn out badly and that we are invested enough to care.

It is getting very late now. The children have swimming practice
early the next day. Rabih waits until Kirsten has finished her con-
sideration of where Esther and William might eventually study,
then reaches over and takes his wife's hand. She lets it lie there
unattended a while, then gives it a squeeze and they begin to kiss.
He opens, and starts to stroke, her thighs. As he's doing so, his
gaze strays to the night-table, on which Kirsten has placed a card
from William: 'Happy Bithrdey Mumy', it says, alongside a drawing of an extremely good-natured and smiley sun. This makes him
think of William's impish face and, also, of Kirsten taking him on
her shoulders around the kitchen, which she did only the previous
week, when he'd dressed up as a wizard after school.

One part of Rabih very much wants to press on with seducing
his wife, he's been wanting this for so long; but another side of him
isn't so sure if he's properly in the mood now, for reasons he finds
hard to pin down.

It's a well-known thesis: the people we are attracted to as adults bear a
marked resemblance to the people we most loved as children. It might
be a certain sense of humour or a kind of expression, a temperament or
an emotional disposition.

Yet there is one thing we want to do with our grown-up lovers that
was previously very much off-limits with our reassuring early caregivers;
we seek to have sex with the very individuals who in key ways remind
us of types with whom we were once strongly expected not *to have sex.*
It follows that successful intercourse depends on shutting down some of
the overly vivid associations between our romantic partners and their
underlying parental archetypes. We need — for a little while — to make

sure our sexual feelings don't become unhelpfully confused with our affectionate ones.

But the task becomes trickier the moment children arrive and directly call upon the specifically parental aspects of our partners. We might be aware at a conscious level that our partner is of course not a sexually forbidden parent, that they're the same person they always were and that, in the early months, we once did fun and transgressive things with them. And yet the idea is put under ever greater strain as their sexual selves grow increasingly obscured beneath the nurturing identities they must wear all day, exemplified by those chaste and sprightly titles (which we might even occasionally mistakenly use to refer to them ourselves): 'Mum' or 'Dad'.

What his wife's breasts might look like was once a subject of inordinate concern for Rabih. He remembers casting surreptitious glances at them in the black top she wore the first time they met, then later studying them beneath a white T-shirt which hinted at their fascinatingly modest size, then brushing against them ever so slightly during that initiatory kiss at the Botanic Garden and then finally, in her old kitchen, circling them with his tongue. His obsession with them in the early days was constant. He wanted her to keep her bra on during lovemaking, alternately pushing it up and pulling it down, so as to keep at a maximum pitch the extraordinary contrast between her clothed and unclothed selves. He would ask her to cup and caress them as she might if he weren't there. He wanted to place his penis between them, as if mere hands were not enough and a more definitive indicator of possession and possibility were required to mark out this previously taboo territory.

And yet now, some years later, they lie next to each other in the marital bed with about as much sexual tension between them as there might be between a pair of leathery grandparents tanning themselves on a Baltic nudist beach.

Arousal seems, in the end, to have very little to do with a state of undress; it draws its energy from the possibility of being granted permission to possess a deeply desirable, once forbidden yet now miraculously available and accessible other. It is an expression of grateful wonder, verging on disbelief, that in a world of isolation and disconnection, the wrists, thighs, earlobes and napes of necks are all there, finally, for us to behold: an extraordinary concept that we want to keep checking up on, perhaps as often as every few hours, once more joyfully touching, inserting, revealing and unclothing, so lonely have we been, so independent and remote have our lovers seemed. Sexual desire is driven by a wish to establish closeness — and is hence contingent on a pre-existing sense of distance, which it is a perpetually distinctive pleasure and relief to try to bridge.

There is very little distance left between Rabih and Kirsten. Their legal status defines them as partners for life; they share a three-by-four-metre bedroom to which they repair every evening; they talk on the phone constantly when they are apart; they are each other's automatically assumed companions every weekend; they know ahead of time, and at most moments of the day and night, exactly what the other is doing. There is no longer very much in their conjoined existence that qualifies as distinctively 'other' – and there is therefore little for the erotic to try to bridge.

At the close of many a day, Kirsten is reluctant even to be touched by Rabih, not because she no longer cares for him, but because she doesn't feel as if there is enough of her left to risk giving more away to another person. One needs a degree of autonomy before being undressed by someone else can feel like a treat. But she has answered too many questions, forced too many small feet into too many shoes, pleaded and cajoled too many times . . . Rabih's touch feels like another hurdle in the way of a long-delayed communion with her neglected interior. She wants to cleave tightly and quietly to herself rather than have her identity be further dispersed across yet more demands. Any advance threatens to destroy the gossamer-thin shell of her private being. Until she has had sufficient chance to reacquaint herself with her own thoughts, she can't even begin to take pleasure in gifting herself to another.

We may, in addition, feel embarrassed and almost intolerably exposed when asking for sex of a partner on whom we are already so deeply dependent in a variety of ways. It can be an intimacy too far, against a backdrop of tense discussions around what to do with the finances and the school drop-off, where to go on holiday and what kind of chair to buy, also to ask that a partner look indulgently upon our sexual needs: that they put on a certain article of clothing, or take part in a dark scenario we crave or lie down in a particular pose on the bed. We may not want to be relegated to the supplicant's role, or to burn up precious emotional capital in the name of a certain fetish. We may prefer not to entrust fantasies which we know can make us look ludicrous or depraved to someone before whom we otherwise have to maintain poise and authority, as required by the daily negotiations and stand-offs of conjugal life. We might find it a lot safer to think about a complete stranger instead.

The week before, Kirsten is alone in the house, up in the bedroom, one mid-afternoon. There's a programme on the television about the North Sea fishing fleet based at Kinlochbervie in the Northwest. We meet the fishermen, hear about their use of new sonar technology and learn about a worrying decline in various piscine populations. At least there's a lot of herring about and the supply of cod isn't too bad this year, either. A fisherman named Clyde captains a boat called the *Loch Davan*. Every week he goes out on the high seas, often venturing as far as Iceland or the tip of Greenland. He has a brutish arrogant manner, a sharp jawline and angry impatient eyes. The children won't be back from their friends' for another hour at least, but Kirsten gets up and shuts the bedroom door tightly nonetheless before taking off her trousers and lying back on the bed.

She's on the *Loch Davan* now, assigned a narrow cabin next to the bridge. There's a fierce wind, rocking the boat like a toy, but above the roar, she can just make out a knocking at the cabin door. It's Clyde; there must be some emergency on the bridge. But it turns out to be a different matter. He rips off her oilskins and takes her against the cabin wall without their exchanging a word. The bristles of his beard burn her skin. He is, crucially, barely literate, extremely coarse, almost pre-verbal and as utterly worthless to her as she is to him. Thinking about the sex feels crude, urgent, meaningless – and very much more exciting than making love in the evening to someone she cares about deeply.

The motif of a beloved taking second place to a random stranger in a masturbatory fantasy has no logical part in Romantic ideology. But in practice it is precisely the dispassionate separation of love and sex that may be needed to correct and relieve the burdens of intimacy. Using a stranger bypasses resentments, emotional vulnerability and any obligation to worry about another's needs. We can be just as peculiar and selfish as we like, without fear of judgement or consequence. All emotion is kept wonderfully at bay; there is not the slightest wish to be understood, and therefore no risk, either, of being misunderstood and, consequently, of growing bitter or frustrated. We can, at last, have desire without needing to bring the rest of our exhaustingly encumbered lives into the bed with us.

Kirsten isn't alone in finding it safer to partition off some bits of her sexuality from the rest of her life. Rabih regularly does a very similar thing. Tonight, he checks that his wife is asleep, whispers her name and hopes she won't answer. Then, when he is sure it is safe, he tiptoes out, thinking he might – after all – make a good murderer, and heads down the stairs, past the children's rooms (he can see his son curled up with Geoffrey, his favourite bear) and to a little annexe off the kitchen, where he navigates to his favourite chat room. It is almost midnight.

Here, too, things are so much easier than with his spouse. There's no need to wonder whether another person is in the mood; you just click on their name and, given the part of the web they're in, assume they will be game.

He also doesn't have to worry, in this milieu, about being normal. This isn't the version of himself which has to do the school run tomorrow, or give a talk at work or later host a dinner party with a few lawyers and a kindergarten teacher and his wife.

He doesn't have to be kind to or care about others. He doesn't even have to belong to his own gender. He can try out what it's like to be a shy, and surprisingly convincing, lesbian from Glasgow, taking her first tentative steps towards a sexual awakening.

And then the moment he's done, he can shut off the machine and return to being the person that so many other people – his children, his spouse and his colleagues – are relying on him to be.

From one perspective, it can seem pathetic to have to concoct fantasies – rather than to try to build a life in which daydreams can reliably become realities. But fantasies are often the best thing we can make of our multiple and contradictory wishes; they allow us to inhabit one reality without destroying the other. Fantasizing spares those we care about from the full irresponsibility and scary strangeness of our urges. It is, in its own way, an achievement, an emblem of civilization – and an act of kindness.

The imaginary incidents on the trawler and in the chat room aren't an indication that Rabih and Kirsten have ceased to love one another. They are signs that the couple are so engaged in each other's lives that they sometimes no longer have the inner freedom to make love without self-consciousness or an inhibiting sense of responsibility.

The Prestige of Laundry

They are a modern couple and therefore share tasks according to a complex arrangement. Rabih goes to work five days a week but comes home early on Friday afternoons to look after the children, which he is also responsible for doing on Saturday mornings and Sunday afternoons. Kirsten works Mondays, Tuesdays and Wednesdays till two o'clock and at weekends is with the kids on Saturday afternoons and Sunday mornings. He does Friday bath time and prepares supper four nights a week. She buys the food and the household supplies, while he takes care of the bins, the car and the garden.

It's just after seven on a Thursday evening. Since this morning Rabih has attended four meetings, dealt with a failing tile supplier, cleared up (he hopes) a misconception about tax rebates and sought to bring the new CFO on board with a scheme for a client conference which could have great implications for the third quarter (or, alternatively, could be a bit of a mess). He has had to stand in the aisle of a crowded commuter bus for half an hour each way and is now walking back from his stop in the rain. He is thinking about how great it will be finally to get home, pour himself a glass of wine, read the children a chapter of *The Famous Five*, kiss them goodnight and sit down for a meal and some civilized conversation with his most sympathetic ally and friend, his spouse. He is at the end of his tether and inclined to feel (justifiably) sorry for himself.

Kirsten has meanwhile been home almost all day. After driving the children to school (there was an ugly fight in the car over a pencil case), she put away breakfast, made the beds, took three work-related calls (her colleagues seem to have a hard time remembering she's not in the office on Thursdays or Fridays), cleaned two bathrooms, vacuumed the house and sorted out everyone's summer clothes. She arranged for a plumber to come and look at the taps, picked up the dry-cleaning and delivered a chair to be reupholstered, booked a dental check-up for William, collected the children from school, prepared and fed them a (healthy) snack, cajoled them into doing their homework, got supper ready, ran a bath and cleaned a set of ink stains off the living-room floor. Now she is thinking how great it will be finally to have Rabih come home and take over, so she can pour herself a glass of wine, read the children a chapter of *The Famous Five*, kiss them goodnight and sit down for a meal and some civilized conversation with her most sympathetic ally and friend, her spouse. She is at the end of her tether and inclined to feel (justifiably) sorry for herself.

When they at last find themselves alone in bed, reading, Kirsten doesn't want to cause trouble, but there are a few things on her mind.

'Will you remember to iron the duvet covers tomorrow?' she asks without raising her eyes from her book.

His stomach twists. He strives for patience. 'It's Friday,' he points out. 'I thought perhaps you could do that kind of thing on a Friday.'

Now she looks up. Her gaze is cold. 'Gotcha, gotcha,' she says.

'Domestic stuff: my job. Never mind. Sorry I asked.' Back to her book.

These grating, scratching encounters can be more exhausting than flat-out rage.

He thinks: I now earn two-thirds of our income, possibly even more depending on how the total is calculated, but it seems I also do more than my fair share of everything else. I'm made to feel as though my work is solely something I am doing for me. In fact, it's rarely satisfying and invariably stressful. I can't be expected, on top of it all, to take on the duvets. I do my bit: I took the children swimming last weekend and just now I loaded the dishwasher. Deep down, I want to be nurtured and protected. I'm furious.

And she thinks: Everyone seems to believe my two days at home are all about 'relaxing' and that I'm lucky to have this time. But this family wouldn't hold together for five minutes without all the things I get done in the background. Everything is my responsibility. I long to take a break, but whenever I bring up some chore I want to pass on, I'm made to feel I'm being unfair – so, in the end, it seems easier to be quiet. There's something wrong with the lights again and I will have to chase the electrician tomorrow. Deep down, I want to be nurtured and protected. I'm furious.

The modern expectation is that there will be equality in all things in the couple, which means, at heart, an equality of suffering. But calibrating grief to ensure an equal dosage is no easy task; misery is experienced subjectively, and there is always a temptation for each party to form a sincere yet competitive conviction that, in truth, his or her life really is more cursed – in ways that the partner seems uninclined to acknowledge or atone for. It takes a superhuman wisdom to avoid the consoling conclusion that one has the harder life.

Kirsten goes to work for enough hours of the week and earns enough money to feel uninclined to be overly grateful to Rabih just for his slightly greater salary. At the same time, Rabih has taken on enough tasks around the house and has been left to fend for himself on enough evenings to feel uninclined to be overly grateful to Kirsten just for her greater efforts around the children. Both are engaged with a sufficient share of the other's primary task not to be in any mood for unalloyed gratitude.

The difficulties of modern parents can in part be blamed on the way prestige is distributed. Couples are not only besieged by practical demands at every hour, they are also inclined to think of these demands as humiliating, banal and meaningless, and are therefore likely to be averse to offering pity or praise to one another, or themselves, just for enduring them. The word 'prestige' sounds wholly inappropriate when applied to the school run and the laundry because we have been perniciously trained to think of this quality as naturally belonging elsewhere, in high politics or scientific research, the movies or fashion. But stripped to its essence, prestige merely refers to whatever is most noble and important in life.

We seem unwilling to allow for the possibility that the glory of our species may lie not only in the launch of satellites, the founding of companies and the manufacture of miraculously thin semi-conductors, but also in an ability — even if it is widely distributed among billions — to spoon yoghurt into small mouths, find missing socks, clean toilets, deal with tantrums and wipe congealed things off tables. Here, too, there are trials worthy not of condemnation or sarcastic ridicule but of a degree of glamour, so that they may be endured with greater sympathy and fortitude.

Rabih and Kirsten are suffering partly because they have so seldom seen their struggles sympathetically reflected in the art they know, which instead tends to belittle and poke puerile fun at the sorts of troubles they face. They cannot admire their own valour in trying to teach a foreign language to a child who is squirming in impatient fury; in constantly buttoning coats and keeping track of hats; in decently maintaining a household; in controlling and mastering moods of despair; and in helping to pull their modest but complicated domestic enterprise along with every new day. They will never be outwardly distinguished or earn large sums of money, they will die in obscurity and without the laurels of their community, and yet the good order and continuity of civilization nevertheless depend to some tiny but vital degree on their quiet, unnoticed labours.

Were Rabih and Kirsten able to read about themselves as characters in a novel, they might – if the author had even a little talent – experience a brief but helpful burst of pity at their not at all unworthy plight, and thereby perhaps learn to dissolve some of the tension that arises on those evenings when, once the children are in bed, the apparently demoralizing and yet in truth deeply grand and significant topic of the ironing comes up.

ADULTERY

Love Rat

Rabih is invited to Berlin to give a talk about public space at a conference on urban regeneration. He changes planes in London and flips through a succession of magazines over Germany. Prussia lies flat and vast below, under a light dusting of November snow.

The event is taking place east of the city, in a conference centre with an adjoining hotel. His room, on the twentieth floor, is clinically austere and white, with views on to a canal and rows of allotments. At night, which comes early, he can see a power station and a procession of pylons striding into the distance in the direction of the Polish border.

At the welcome drinks party in the ballroom, he knows no one and pretends to be waiting for a colleague. Once back in his room, he calls home. The children have just had their baths. 'I like it when you're away,' says Esther. 'Mummy's letting us watch a film and have a pizza.' Rabih stares at a single-engine plane circling high above the frozen fields beyond the hotel's car park. As Esther talks, William can be heard singing in the background, making a show of how uninterested he is in any father who has had the bad taste to leave him behind. Their voices sound younger over the telephone; it would be eerie for them to know just how much he misses them.

He eats a club sandwich while looking at a news channel, through whose lenses a series of tragedies appears relentlessly uniform and unengaging.

At dawn the following day he practises his speech in front of the bathroom mirror. The real thing happens at eleven in the main hall. He makes his points with passion and a deep knowledge of his subject. It's his life's work to champion the virtues of well-designed shared spaces which can bring a community together. A number of people come up to congratulate him afterwards. At lunch he's seated at a table with delegates from around the world. It's been a while since he's experienced an atmosphere this cosmopolitan. There's a hostile conversation in progress about America. A Pakistani working in Qatar decries the impact of America's zoning laws on turning circles; a Dutchman alleges an indifference on the part of the nation's elites towards the common good; a Finnish delegate compares its citizens' dependence on fossil fuels with an addict's relationship to opium.

At the end of the table a woman is leaning her head to one side, sporting a wry, resigned smile.

'I know better than to try to defend my country when I'm overseas,' she interjects eventually. 'Of course, I'm every bit as disappointed in America as the rest of you are, but I still have a deep sense of loyalty to it – just as I might with some crazy alcoholic aunt whom I'd stick up for if I heard strangers talking about her behind her back.'

Lauren lives in Los Angeles and works at UCLA, where she's studying the effects of immigration in the San Bernardino Valley. She has shoulder-length brown hair, grey-green eyes and is thirty-one. Rabih tries not to look at her too directly.

Hers is the sort of beauty that seems unhelpful to encounter in his present circumstances.

There's an hour before the sessions start again and he decides to take a walk outside, in what passes for a garden. His flight home departs early the next morning and there'll be a new project waiting on his desk when he gets back to Edinburgh. Lauren's dark, tailored dress did nothing to draw attention to itself and yet he remembers every detail of it. He thinks, too, of the stack of bangles on her left arm; he could just see a tattoo underneath them, on the inside of her wrist – an inadvertent, melancholy reminder of the generation gap between them.

In the late afternoon, in the corridor leading to the lifts, he's looking at some brochures when she walks by. He smiles awkwardly, grieving already that he will never know her, that her deeper identity (symbolized by the purple canvas bag slung over her shoulder) will remain forever foreign to him, that he can write himself only a single life. But she announces that she's feeling hungry and suggests that he join her for tea in a wood-panelled bar next to the business centre on the first floor. She had breakfast there that morning, she adds. They sit on a long leather bench by the fireplace. There is a white orchid behind Lauren. He asks most of the questions and thereby learns bits and pieces: about her apartment in Venice Beach, a previous job at a university in Arizona, the family in Albuquerque, her love of David Lynch's films, her involvement in community organizing, her Judaism and her hammed-up terror of German officials, which extends also to the stiff and thick-necked barman, a character rich in comedic possibilities, whom she nicknames Eichmann. Rabih's attention wavers between the specifics of what she's saying and what she represents. She is at once herself and all the people he has ever admired but learned not to be curious about since his wedding day.

Her eyes crinkle with laughter as she glances up at the barman.

' "You'll never turn the vinegar to jam, Mein Herr!" ' she sings under her breath, and Rabih's own breath catches in wonder at her charm. He feels fifteen again and she is Alice Saure.

She flew into Frankfurt the day before and took the train here, she tells him; she finds European trains so good for thinking. Rabih realizes it must now be close to bath time back at home. How simple it would be to explode his life simply by moving his hand ten centimetres to the left.

'Tell me about you,' she prompts. Well, he studied in London, then went up to Edinburgh; work keeps him busy, though he likes to travel when he can; yes, he does rather mind the gloomy weather, but perhaps it's a useful discipline not to worry too much about the state of the skies. The editing comes with unexpected ease. 'What did you do today, Daddy?' he hears his children enquiring. Daddy gave a talk in front of lots of people, then read his book for a while and had an early night so he can take the first plane home tomorrow to see his darling girl and special boy – who might as well not exist right now.

'I can't face the delegates' dinner,' she says at seven, after Eichmann returns to ask if they would like a cocktail now.

So they walk out of the bar together. His hands are trembling as he presses the button for the lift. He asks what floor she needs and stands opposite her in the see-through glass cubicle on its way up. A fog has settled over the landscape.

The forthrightness of the middle-aged seducer is rarely a matter of confidence or arrogance; it is instead a species of impatient despair born of a pitiful awareness of the ever-increasing proximity of death.

In its basic form, her room is nearly identical to his, but he is surprised by how different its atmosphere seems. A purple dress is hanging on one wall and a catalogue from the Neues Museum has been set down by the television; there's an open laptop on the desk, there are two postcards of a painting of Goethe near the mirror and, on the night-table, her phone is docked into the hotel stereo. She asks if he has heard of a certain singer and summons up her album with a few taps: the arrangement is spare, just a piano and some percussion in what sounds like a cavernous cathedral, and then a powerful female voice cuts in, haunting, unusually deep and then suddenly high and fragile. 'I especially love this part,' she says, and then closes her eyes for a moment. He remains standing next to the foot of the bed as the singer repeats the word *always* in rising octaves, like a cry that goes straight to his soul. He has kept clear of such music since the children were born. It serves no good purpose to be transported like this when the confines of his life demand resoluteness and impassivity.

He goes to her, takes her face in his hands and puts his lips to hers. She draws him close and shuts her eyes again. 'I will give you everything . . .' sings the voice.

It happens much as he remembers it from before, that first span with someone new. If he could collect every such scene from across his past and put them together on a single loop, the total running time might be no more than half an hour, yet these would in many ways be the finest moments of his life.

It feels as if he has been granted access to a version of himself which he had long thought dead.

What dangers are posed by those touchingly insecure men who, unsure of their own powers of attraction, need to keep finding out whether they are acceptable to others.

She turns down the lights. There are so many differences within the same basic parameters: her tongue more curious and impatient, her back arching just as he moves to her stomach, her legs tauter, her thighs darker. What would stop him now? The idea that all of this is wrong has moved away into the far distance, like an alarm bell ringing through a deep sleep.

They lie still afterwards, their breathing slowly calming itself. The curtains are open, providing a view of the brightly illuminated power station in the fog.

'What's your wife like?' she asks, smiling.

It's impossible to judge her tone of voice or to know how to answer. His and Kirsten's challenges feel too distinctly their own to share, even if they have now attracted a new, more innocent satellite into their orbit.

'She's . . . nice.' He falters.

Lauren maintains her inscrutable expression but doesn't press. He caresses her shoulder; somewhere, through a wall, a lift can be heard descending. He can't claim to be bored at home. It's not that he doesn't respect his wife, nor even that he doesn't desire her any more. No, the truth of his situation is more peculiar and more humiliating. He is in love with a woman who too often appears not to need love at all; a fighter so capable and strong that there are few opportunities afforded to nurture her; someone with a problematic relationship to anyone inclined to help her, and who sometimes seems most comfortable when she feels disappointed by those to whom she has entrusted herself. It appears he has had sex with Lauren for no greater or lesser reason than that he and his wife have of late been finding it extremely hard to have a hug – and that he is, somewhere inside, without much justice, really rather hurt by, and furious about, the fact.

It's rare to embark on an affair out of indifference to a spouse. One gener-
ally has to care quite a lot about a partner to bother to betray them.

'I think you'd like her,' he finally adds.

'I'm sure I would,' she answers evenly. Now her look is mischievous.

They order room service. She wants pasta with lemon and a little Parmesan on the side; she seems used to explaining such requirements with precision to people who will care. Rabih, easily intimidated in service contexts, admires her sense of entitlement. The phone rings and she takes a call from a colleague in Los Angeles, where it's still late morning.

Perhaps even more than the sex itself, it is the intimacy possible in its wake which draws him in. It is a quirk of the age that the easiest way to start a friendship with someone is generally by asking them to get undressed.

They are warm towards and considerate of each other. Neither will have a chance to let the other down. They can both appear competent, generous, trustworthy and believable, as strangers will. She laughs at his jokes. His accent is kind of irresistible, she says. It makes him feel a little lonely to realize how easy it is to be liked by someone who has no idea who he is.

They talk until midnight, then fall asleep chastely on opposite sides of the bed. In the morning they travel together to the airport and have a coffee at the check-in area.

'Stay in touch – as much as you can.' She smiles. 'You're one of the good guys.'

They hug tightly, expressing the pure affection available only to two people who have no further designs upon each other. Their lack of time is a privilege. Under its aegis they can each remain forever impressive in the other's eyes. He feels tears welling up and attempts to compose himself by staring at a watch advertised by a fighter pilot. With the prospect of an ocean and a continent between them, he is free to let loose all his aspirations for closeness. Both can ache with a desire for intimacy and be protected from any of its consequences. They will never have to be resentful; they can continue to appreciate each other as only those without a future can.

Pro

He makes it home early on Saturday afternoon. To his surprise, the world appears to be carrying on much as it has always done. No one stares at him at the airport or on the bus. Edinburgh is intact. The front-door key still works. Kirsten is in the study helping William with his homework. This accomplished, intelligent woman, who has a first-class degree from Aberdeen University, who is a member of the Scottish chapter of the Royal Institution of Chartered Surveyors and daily handles budgets in the millions, has been ordered to sit on the floor by a seven-and-a-half-year-old boy, who holds an unparalleled command over her and is just now impatiently urging her to colour in some archers in his version of the Battle of Flodden Field.

Rabih has presents for everyone (bought on the other side of passport control). He tells Kirsten he can take over with the children, prepare supper and do bath time; he's sure she must be exhausted. An impure conscience is a useful spur to being a bit nicer.

Rabih and Kirsten go to bed early. She has, for an age, been his first port of call for every piece of news, however trivial or grave. How odd it seems, therefore, for him to be in possession of information at once so significant and yet so deeply resistant to the customary principles of disclosure.

It would be almost natural to start by explaining how curious it was that he and Lauren happened to bump into each other by the lifts – since he was scheduled to be at a talk at the time – and how touching he found it when, after their lovemaking, she haltingly described the illness and death of a grandmother to whom she had been unusually close throughout her childhood. Adopting the same easy, digressive approach they take when picking apart the psychology of people they meet at parties or the plotlines of films they see together, they might review how moving and sad it was for Rabih to say goodbye to Lauren at Tegel Airport, and how thrilling and (a little) scary to receive a text from her on landing. There could be no one better qualified to consider such themes with than his insightful, inquisitive, funny and observant co-explorer of existence.

It is a bit of a job, therefore, to keep reminding himself how close he is to unleashing a tragedy. Esther apparently has a play-date the following morning at an indoor ski slope. This is where their story could come to a decisive end, and madness and mayhem begin. They will have to leave the house at nine to be there by a quarter to ten. It would, he is aware, take only a sentence to bring everything settled and coherent in his current life to a close: his brain contains a piece of information a mere six or so words long which is capable of blowing the household sky-high. Their daughter will need her gloves, which are in that box in the attic marked 'Winter Clothes'. He marvels at the mind's capacity not to let slip a single outward indication of the dynamite it contains. All the same, he is tempted to check in the bathroom mirror to make sure that nothing is leaking out of him.

He understands – for the idea has been drummed into him from an early age by society – that what he has done is wrong. Very wrong indeed. He is, in the language of the tabloids, a scumbag, a love rat, a cheat and a traitor. Nevertheless, he also registers that the exact nature of the ill he has committed is not in fact entirely clear to him. He does feel some concern, but for cautionary, secondary reasons – that is, because he wants tomorrow to go well, and the days and years thereafter. In his depths, however, he can't find it in himself to believe that what has happened in the Berlin hotel room is truly bad in and of itself. Is this perhaps, he wonders, just the eternal excuse of the love rat?

Through the lens of Romanticism there can be, quite simply, no greater betrayal. Even for those willing to countenance almost every other kind of behaviour, adultery remains the one seismic transgression, appalling in its violation of a series of the most sacred assumptions of love.

The first of these is that one person can't possibly claim to love another – and by implication in any way value their life together – and then slip off and have sex with someone else. If such a disaster were to happen, it could only be that there had been no love to begin with.

Kirsten has fallen asleep. He brushes a strand of hair from her forehead. He recalls how differently responsive were Lauren's ears and her belly, even through her dress. By the time they were at the bar, it looked as if something was going to happen between them; it became a certainty the moment she asked if he came to these conferences often, and he replied that this already felt like a very unusual one, and she smiled warmly. Her directness was the centrepiece of her enchantment. 'This is nice,' she turned around and said when they were in bed, as though trying out some unfamiliar dish in a restaurant. But the mind has many chambers, and a dazzling capacity for building firewalls. In another zone, another galaxy entirely, there remains untouched the love he has for Kirsten's way of telling rude jokes at parties, the surprising trove of poems she keeps in her head (Coleridge and Burns), her habit of pairing black skirts and tights with trainers, her skill at unblocking a sink and her knowledge of what might be going on under a car bonnet (the sorts of things which women let down by their fathers at a young age seem to be particularly good at). There's no one on earth he'd rather have dinner with than his wife, who is also his best friend. Which hasn't, however, in any way prevented him from possibly ruining her life.

A second assumption: adultery isn't just any old kind of disloyalty. A transgression involving nakedness is of a fundamentally different order, says the world; it's a betrayal of a cataclysmic and incomparable sort. Screwing around is not somewhat bad, it's the very worst thing one person could do to another whom he or she claims to love.

This wasn't – clearly – exactly what Kirsten McLelland signed up to, many years ago, in that salmon-pink register office in Inverness. Then again, there have been a number of things over the course of their marriage that Rabih Khan didn't anticipate, either, including his wife's strong objection to his wish to return to architecture, primarily because she didn't want their income to be curtailed for even a few months; her cutting him off from many of his friends because she found them 'boring'; her tendency to make jokes at his expense in company; the blame he has to shoulder when things go wrong at her work; and the exhausting anxiety she suffers over every aspect of their children's education . . . These are the stories he has told himself, lines of reasoning that are simpler than wondering if he may have held *himself* back in his career or if his friends really might not be quite as entertaining as they seemed when he was twenty-two.

Still, Rabih questions whether that half an hour should so

conclusively shift the moral calculation against him, if it should on its own be what commits him to fiery damnation. While they may lack the same power to stir up ready indignation, there are betrayals of an equally damaging (if less visible) sort in her habits of not listening, of failing to forgive, of casting unfair blame, and in her casual belittlement and her stretches of indifference. He doesn't want to add up the ledger, but he isn't sure that on the basis of this single, admittedly deeply wounding act, he ought so easily and definitively to qualify as the villain of the entire piece.

A third assumption: a commitment to monogamy is an admirable consequence of love, stemming from a deep-seated generosity and an intimate interest in the other's flourishing and well-being. A call for monogamy is a sure indication that one partner has the other's best interests at heart.

To Rabih's new way of thinking, it seems anything *but* kind or considerate to insist that a spouse return to his room alone to watch CNN and eat yet another club sandwich while perched on the edge of his bed, when he has perhaps only a few more decades of life left on the planet, an increasingly dishevelled physique, an at best intermittent track record with the opposite sex, and a young woman from California standing before him who sincerely wishes to remove her dress in his honour.

If love is to be defined as a genuine concern for the well-being of another person, then it must surely be deemed compatible with granting permission for an often harassed and rather browbeaten husband to step off the elevator on the eighteenth floor, in order to enjoy ten minutes of rejuvenating cunnilingus with a near-stranger. Otherwise it may seem that what we are dealing with is not really love at all but rather a kind of small-minded and hypocritical possessiveness, a desire to make one's partner happy if, but only if, that happiness involves oneself.

It's past midnight already, yet Rabih is just hitting his stride, knowing there might be objections but sidestepping them nimbly and, in the process, acquiring an ever more brittle sense of self-righteousness.

A fourth assumption: monogamy is the natural state of love. A sane person can only ever want to love one other person. Monogamy is the bellwether of emotional health.

Is there not, wonders Rabih, an infantile idealism in our wish to find everything in one other being – someone who will be simultaneously a best friend, a lover, a co-parent, a co-chauffeur and a business partner? What a recipe for disappointment and resentment in this notion, upon which millions of otherwise perfectly good marriages regularly founder.

What could be more natural than to feel an occasional desire for another person? How can anyone be expected to grow up in hedonistic, liberated circles, experience the sweat and excitement of nightclubs and summer parks, listen to music full of longing and lust and then, immediately upon signing a piece of paper, renounce all outside sexual interest, not in the name of any particular god or higher commandment but merely from an unexplored supposition that it must be very wrong? Is there not instead something inhuman, indeed 'wrong', in *failing* to be tempted, in failing to realize just how short of time we all are and therefore with what urgent curiosity we should want to explore the unique fleshly individuality of more than one of our contemporaries? To moralize against adultery is to deny the legitimacy of a range of sensory high points – Rabih thinks of Lauren's shoulder blades – in their own way just as worthy of reverence as more acceptable attractions such as the last moments of 'Hey Jude' or the ceilings of the Alhambra Palace. Isn't the rejection of adulterous possibilities tantamount to an infidelity towards the richness of life itself? To turn the equation on its head: would it be rational to trust anyone who *wasn't*, under certain circumstances, really pretty interested in being unfaithful?

Contra

The texts are, at first, purely civil. Did he get back safely? How is her jet lag? Some professional themes come into it, too: has he received the post-conference newsletter? Does she know the work of the urbanist Jan Gehl?

Then, at eleven one night, he feels his phone vibrate and goes into the bathroom. From Los Angeles she has written that she is, truth be told, finding it hard to forget his cock.

He deletes the message at once, takes out the phone's SIM card and hides it in his washbag, stashes the phone under a tracksuit and goes back to bed. Kirsten stretches her arms out towards him. The next day, with the phone reassembled, he sends Lauren a return text from the laundry cupboard under the stairs: 'Thanks for an extraordinary, wonderful, generous night. I won't ever regret it. I think of your vagina.' For a number of reasons, he deletes the last sentence before sending.

As for the never regretting, in reality, surrounded by drying towels, it's starting to feel rather more complicated.

The following Saturday, in a toy shop in the centre of town where he has gone with William to buy a model boat, an email arrives with an attachment. Beside a shelf full of small sails, he reads: 'I love your name, Rabih Khan. Every time I say it out loud to myself, it satisfies me somehow. And yet it also makes me sad, because it reminds me how much time I've wasted with men who don't share your genuine and passionate nature, and who haven't been able to understand the parts of me that I need to have under-stood. I hope you'll like the attached photo of me in my favourite Oxfords and socks. It's the real me, the one I'm so thrilled to know you saw and may see again before too long.'

William tugs at his jacket. There's dismay in his voice: the boat he's been obsessing about all month costs far more than he antici-pated. Rabih feels himself go pale. The self-portrait shows her standing in a bathroom, facing a full-length mirror with her head angled to one side, wearing nothing but lace-up shoes and a pair of knee-high yellow and black socks. He offers to buy William a toy aircraft carrier.

The message stays unanswered for the rest of the weekend. He has no time or opportunity to come back to it until the Monday night, when Kirsten is out at her book club.

When he opens his email app to reply, he sees that Lauren has got there first: 'I know your situation is difficult, and I'd never want to do anything to jeopardize it – but I was just feeling so vulnerable and silly that night. I don't usually send naked pictures of myself to men I hardly know. I was a little hurt by your non-response. Forgive me for saying that – I know I've got no right. I just keep thinking of your kind, sweet face. You're a good man, Rabih. Don't let anyone ever tell you otherwise. I like you more than I should. I want you inside me now.'

For the sweet-faced man, things are feeling ever more tricky.

Perhaps not coincidentally, Rabih becomes increasingly aware of his wife's goodness. He notices the trouble she takes with nearly everything she does. Every night she spends hours helping the children with their homework; she remembers their spelling tests, rehearses lines for school plays with them and sews patches on to their trousers. She's sponsoring an orphan with a lip deformation in Malawi. Rabih develops an ulcer on the inside of his cheek and, without being asked, his wife buys a healing gel and drops it off for him at work. She is doing a fine job of appearing to be a great deal nicer than he is, which he is both extremely grateful for and, on another level, utterly furious about.

Her generosity seems to show up the extent of his inadequacy and grows less tolerable by the day. His behaviour declines. He snaps at her in front of the children. He drags his heels about doing the bins and the linen. He wishes she would be a little bit awful back to him, in order that her assessment of him might appear better aligned with his own sense of self-worth.

Late one evening, after they've gone to bed and while Kirsten is relaying something about the car's annual service, his discomfort reaches a pitch.

'Oh, and I had the tyres realigned – apparently you need to do that every six months or so,' she says, not even glancing up from her reading.

'Kirsten, why would you ever bother with that?'

'Well, it might matter. It can be dangerous not to do it, the mechanic said.'

'You're frightening, you know.'

' "Frightening"?'

'The way you're so . . . so *organized*, such a *planner*, so god-damned reasonable about everything.'

' "Reasonable"?'

'Everything around here is deeply sensible, rational, worked out, policed – as if there were a timetable all laid out from now till the moment we die.'

'I don't understand,' Kirsten says. Her expression is one of pure puzzlement. 'Policed? I went to have the car fixed, and at once I'm a villain in some anti-bourgeois narrative you've got running through your head?'

'Yes, you're right. You're always right. I just wonder why you're such a genius at making me feel I'm the mad, horrible one. All I can say is, everything is very well ordered around here.'

'I thought you liked order.'

'I thought so, too.'

' "Thought", past tense?'

'It can start to seem dead. Boring, even.' He can't help himself. He's impelled to say the very worst things, to try to smash the relationship to see if it's real and worth trusting.

'You're not putting this very nicely at all. And I don't think anything around here is boring. I wish it were.'

'It is. *I've* become boring. And you've become boring, too, in case you hadn't noticed.'

Kirsten stares straight ahead of her, her eyes wider than usual. She rises from the bed with silent dignity, her finger still in the book she has been reading, and walks out of the room. He hears her go down the stairs and then shut the living-room door behind her.

'Why do you have to have such a talent for making me feel so damned guilty about everything I do?' he calls after her. 'St *fucking* Kirsten . . .' And he stamps his foot on the floor with sufficient force briefly to wake up his daughter in the room below.

Twenty minutes of rumination later, he follows Kirsten downstairs. She is sitting in the armchair, by the lamp, with a blanket around her shoulders. She doesn't look up when he enters. He sits down on the sofa and puts his head in his hands. Next door in the kitchen the fridge lets off an audible shiver as its thermostat kicks the motor on.

'You think it's fun for me, all this, do you?' she says eventually, still without looking at him. 'Throwing the best parts of my career away in order to manage two constantly exhausting, maddening, beautiful children and an oh-so-interesting on-the-verge-of-a-nervous-breakdown husband? Do you think this is what I dreamed of when I was fifteen and read Germaine Greer's bloody *Female Eunuch*? Do you know how much nonsense I have to fill my head with every day of the week just so this household can function? And meanwhile, all you can do is harbour some mysterious resentment about my supposedly having prevented you from reaching your full potential as an architect, when the truth is that you yourself worry about money far more than I do, except you find it useful to blame me for your own caution. Because it's always so much easier if it's *my* fault. I ask one thing and one thing only from you – that you treat me with respect. I don't care what you daydream about or what you may get up to when you go here and there, but I will *not* tolerate your being uncivil towards me. You think you're the only one who gets bored of all this now and then? Let me tell you, I'm not constantly thrilled by it, either. In case it hasn't occurred to you, there are times when I feel a little dissatisfied myself – and I certainly don't want *you* policing *me* any more than you want me doing the same to you.'

Rabih stares at her, surprised by the end of her speech.

' "Policing", really?' he asks. 'That's an odd choice of word.'

'You used it first.'

'I didn't.'

'You did, in the bedroom. You said everything here was sensible and policed.'

'I'm sure I didn't.' Rabih pauses. 'Have you done anything that I ought to be policing you about?'

The heartbeat of their relationship, which has been going

non-stop since the afternoon in the Botanic Garden, appears to pause.

'Yes, I'm fucking all the men on the team, every last one of them. I'm glad you finally asked. I thought you never would. At least *they* know how to be civil towards me.'

'*Are* you having an affair?'

'Don't be ridiculous. I have *lunch* with them occasionally.'

'All of them at once?'

'No, Detective Inspector, I prefer one at a time.'

Rabih is slumped at the table, which is covered with the children's homework. Kirsten paces by the larder, to which is tacked a large picture of the four of them on a memorably enjoyable holiday in Normandy.

'Which ones do you have lunch with?'

'Why does it matter? All right: Ben McGuire, for one, up in Dundee. He's calm, he likes to go walking, he doesn't seem to think it's such a terrible flaw that I'm "reasonable". Anyway, to get back to the larger point, how can I make it any clearer? Being nice is not boring. It's an enormous achievement, one that 99 per cent of humanity can't manage from day to day. If "nice" is boring, then I love boring. I want you never again to shout at me in front of the children the way you did yesterday. I don't like men who shout. There's nothing charming about it at all. I thought the whole point of you was that you didn't shout.'

Kirsten gets up and goes to fetch a glass of water.

Ben McGuire. The name rings a bell. She's mentioned him before. She went to Dundee for the afternoon once – when was that? There was some sort of council get-together, she said. How dare this McGuire fellow invite his wife to lunch? Is he entirely out of his mind? And without even asking Rabih's permission, which he would certainly never have given.

He begins his inquisition at once: 'Kirsten, have you done anything with Ben McGuire, or has he otherwise indicated that he
would like in some way to do something to – or should I say
with – you?'

'Don't adopt that strange, detached, lawyerly tone with me,
Rabih. Do you think I'd be talking like this with you if I had something to hide? Just because somebody finds me attractive, I'm not
the narcissistic type who feels immediately forced to strip off. But
if someone does actually think I am rather terrific, and if he notices
that I've had my hair cut or admires what I'm wearing, I don't hold
it against him, either. Surprisingly, I am not a virgin. You'll find
that very few women my age are, these days. It's probably even
time you came to terms with the fact that your mother wasn't the
Madonna she lives on as in your imagination. What do you think
she was doing with her evenings when she flew around the world –
reading selected passages of the Gideon Bible in her hotel room?
Whatever it was, I hope for her sake that it was wonderful and that
her lovers adored her – and I'm glad she had the decency never to
involve you in any of it. Bless her. Except that she gave you, through
no fault of her own, some very skewed views about women. Yes,
women do in fact have needs of their own, and sometimes, even if
they have husbands they love and are good mothers, they would
like someone new and unknown to notice them and want them
desperately. Which doesn't mean they won't also be the picture of
sensible concern every day and think about what kinds of healthy
snacks to pack inside their children's lunch boxes. Sometimes you
seem to believe you're the only one around here who has an inner
life. But all of your very subtle feelings are in the end very normal,
and no sign of genius. This is what marriage is and what we signed
up to, both of us, for life, with our eyes open. I intend to be loyal
to that, as much as I can, and I hope you will be, too.'

With that she falls silent. On the counter next to where she's standing there's a large pack of flour, brought out from the pantry in anticipation of a cake she'll make with the children the next day. She stares at it for a moment.

'And as for your complaint that I never do anything crazy . . .' The pack is across the room before he can say a word, striking the wall with such vehemence that it explodes into a white cloud, which takes a surprisingly long time to settle across the dining table and chairs.

'You stupid, hurtful, inadequate man – was that crazy enough for you? Perhaps while you're cleaning it up you'll have time to remember how much fun housework can be. And please don't ever, *ever* call me boring again.'

She goes back upstairs, and Rabih gets down on his knees with the dustpan and brush. There's flour everywhere: it takes nearly a whole roll of paper towels, carefully dampened, to get the bulk of it off the table, off the chairs and out of the crevices in the tiles, and even then he knows that reminders of this event will remain visible for weeks to come. As he works he also recalls, in a way he hasn't done for a while, that he had good reason to marry this particular woman.

It seems especially painful, therefore, to think (erroneously) that he may have lost her to a fellow surveyor from Dundee Council – and, what's worse, just when he has no leg to stand on and no moral authority to exert. Yes, he knows he's being ridiculous, but the thoughts crowd in nevertheless. How long has the adultery been going on? How many times have they met? Where do they do it? In the car? He'll have to check it thoroughly in the morning. He feels nauseous. She is by her very nature so secretive and discreet that she could be carrying on a whole second life, he reflects, without his having a clue. He wouldn't begin to know how to intercept her emails or bug her phone. Does she really even belong to a book club? When she said she was visiting her mother last month, was she actually off for a weekend with her lover? What about the 'coffee' she sometimes has on a Saturday? There might be a tracker he can slip into her coat. He is at once beyond outraged and entirely terrified. His wife is about to leave him, or else she plans to stay but to treat him coldly and angrily for eternity. He misses their past life so much, when all they knew was (he manages to convince himself) calmness, loyalty and stability. He wants to be cradled in her arms like an infant and to turn back the clock. He thought they were going to have a quiet evening, and now everything has come to an end.

To be mature is, we're told, to move beyond possessiveness. Jealousy is for babies. The mature person knows that no one owns anyone. It's what wise people have taught us since our earliest days. Let Jack play with your fire engine: it won't stop being yours if he has a turn. Stop throwing yourself on the floor and thumping your small clenched fists on the carpet in rage. Your little sister may be Daddy's darling, but you're Daddy's darling too. Love isn't like a cake: if you give love to one person, it doesn't mean there is less for anyone else. Love just keeps growing every time there's a new baby in the family.

Later on, the argument makes even more sense around sex. Why would you think ill of a partner if they left you for an hour to go and rub a limited area of their body against that of a stranger? After all, you wouldn't get enraged if they played chess with someone you didn't know or joined a meditation group where they talked intimately of their lives by candlelight, would you?

Rabih can't stop asking certain questions: where was Kirsten last Thursday evening when he called her and got no answer? Who is she trying to impress with her new black shoes? Why, when he types 'Ben McGuire' into the search box on her laptop (which he has fired up in secret in the bathroom), does he get only boring work-related emails between the two of them? How and where else are they communicating? Have they set up hidden email accounts? Is it Skype? Or some new encrypted service? And the most important and stupidest question of all: what's he like in bed?

The stupidity of jealousy makes it a tempting target for those in a moralizing mood. They should spare their breath. However unedifying and plain silly attacks of jealousy may be, they cannot be skirted: we should accept that we simply cannot stay sane on hearing that the person we love and rely on has touched the lips, or even so much as the hand, of another party. This makes no sense, of course – and runs directly counter to the often quite sober and loyal thoughts we may have had when we happened to betray someone in the past. But we are not amenable to reason here. To be wise is to recognize when wisdom will simply not be an option.

He tries consciously to slow down his breathing. It seems as if he might be angry, but at heart he's merely terrified. He tries a technique he once heard described in a magazine: 'Let's imagine what Kirsten, if she *did* have a few experiences with Ben, might have meant by them. What did it mean when I was with Lauren? Did *I* want to abandon Kirsten? Emphatically no. So in all likelihood, when she was with Ben, she didn't want to run off, either. She was probably just feeling ignored and vulnerable and wanted an affirmation of her sexuality – things she's already told me she needs and that I need too. Whatever she may have done was probably no worse than what happened in Berlin, which itself wasn't really so bad. To forgive her would be to come to terms with some of the very same impulses I myself have had, and to see that they were no more the enemies of our marriage and our love for having been hers than mine.'

It sounds very logical and high-minded. Yet it makes no sliver of difference. He is starting to learn about 'being good', but not in the normal, second-hand kind of way, by listening to a sermon or dutifully following social mores from a lack of choice or out of a passive, cowed respect for tradition. He is becoming a slightly nicer person by the most authentic and effective means possible: through having a chance to explore the long-term consequences of bad behaviour from within.

So long as we have been the unconscious beneficiaries of the loyalty of others, sangfroid around adultery comes easily. Never having been betrayed sets up poor preconditions for remaining faithful. Evolving into genuinely more loyal people requires us to suffer through some properly inoculative episodes, in which we feel for a time limitlessly panicked, violated and on the edge of collapse. Only then can the injunction not to betray our spouses evolve from a bland bromide into a permanently vivid moral imperative.

Irreconcilable Desires

He longs, first, for safety. Sunday nights in winter often feel particularly cosy somehow, with the four of them seated around the table eating Kirsten's pasta, William giggling, Esther singing. It's dark outside. Rabih has his favourite German pumpernickel bread. Afterwards there's a game of Monopoly, a pillow fight, then a bath, a story and bedtime for the children. Kirsten and Rabih climb into bed, too, to watch a film; they hold hands under the duvet, just as they did at the start, though now the rest is down to an almost embarrassed peck on the lips as the end credits roll, and both are asleep ten minutes later, secure and cocooned.

But he yearns, also, for adventure. Six thirty on those rare, perfect summer evenings in Edinburgh, when the streets smell of diesel, coffee, fried foods, hot tarmac and sex. The pavements are crowded with people in cotton print dresses and loose-fitting jeans. Everyone sensible is heading home; but for those sticking around, the night promises warmth, intrigue and mischief. A young person in a tight top passes by (perhaps a student or a tourist) and confides the briefest of conspiratorial smiles, and in an instant everything seems within reach. In the coming hours, people will enter bars and discos, shout to make themselves heard over the throb of the music and, buoyed by alcohol and adrenalin, will end up entwined with strangers in the shadows. Rabih is expected back at the house to begin the children's bath time in fifteen minutes.

Our romantic lives are fated to be sad and incomplete, because we are creatures driven by two essential desires which point powerfully in entirely opposing directions. Yet what is worse is our utopian refusal to countenance the divergence, our naive hope that a cost-free synchronization might somehow be found: that the libertine might live for adventure while avoiding loneliness and chaos. Or that the married Romantic might unite sex with tenderness, and passion with routine.

Lauren texts Rabih to ask if they might speak online sometime. She would like to hear and ideally see him again: words just aren't enough.

There's a wait of ten days before Kirsten has something planned that will take her out of the house at night. The children keep him busy until it's nearly time, and then, due to a weak wi-fi signal, he's confined to the kitchen for the duration of the call. He has already checked to make sure, repeatedly, that neither Esther nor William is in need of a glass of water, but he turns to look at the door every few minutes anyway, just in case.

He's never used Facetime before, and it takes a while for him to get it set up. Two women are now in different ways relying on him. A few minutes and three passwords later, Lauren is suddenly there, as if she'd been waiting inside the computer all along.

'I miss you,' she says right away. It's a sunny morning in Southern California.

She's sitting in her kitchen-living room, wearing a casual blue striped top. She's just washed her hair. Her eyes are playful and alive.

'I made coffee. Do you want some?' she asks.

'Sure, and some toast.'

'You like it with butter, I seem to remember? Coming right up.'

The screen flickers for an instant. This is how love affairs will be conducted when we've colonized Mars, he thinks.

Infatuations aren't delusions. That way a person has of holding their head may truly indicate someone confident, wry and sensitive; they really may have the humour and intelligence implied by their eyes and the tenderness suggested by their mouth. The error of the infatuation is more subtle: a failure to keep in mind the central truth of human nature that everyone – not merely our current partners, in whose multiple failings we are such experts – but everyone *will have something substantially and maddeningly wrong with them when we spend more time around them, something so wrong as to make a mockery of those initially rapturous feelings.*

The only people who can still strike us as normal are those we don't yet know very well. The best cure for love is to get to know them better.

When the image returns, he can just make out, in a far corner, what looks to be a drying rack with a few pairs of socks hung on it.

'By the way, where's the reach-over-and-touch-your-lover button on this thing?' she wonders aloud.

He's very much at her mercy. All she would need to do was look up his wife's email on the Edinburgh Council website and drop her a line.

'It's right here on mine,' he replies.

In an instant, his mind shoots forward to a possible future with Lauren. He imagines living with her in LA, in that apartment, after the divorce. They would make love on the couch, he would cradle her in his arms, they'd stay up late talking about their vulnerabilities and longings, and would drive over to Malibu to eat shrimp at a little place she'd know by the ocean. But they'd also need to put out the laundry, wonder who would fix the fuses and get cross because the milk had run out.

It's in part because he likes her a lot that he really doesn't want this to go any further. He knows himself well enough to realize how unhappy he would ultimately make her. In light of all he understands about himself and the course of love, he can see that the kindest thing he can do to someone he truly likes is to get out of the way fast.

Marriage: a deeply peculiar and ultimately unkind thing to inflict on anyone one claims to care for.

'I miss you,' she says again.

'Likewise. I'm also intently staring at your laundry back there over your shoulder. It's very pretty.'

'You mean and perverted man!'

To develop this love story – one logical consequence of his enthusiasm – would in reality end up being the most self-centred and uncaring thing he could do to Lauren, quite aside from to his wife. Real generosity, he recognizes, means admiring, seeing through the urge for permanence and walking away.

'There's something I've been meaning to say . . .' Rabih begins.

As he talks through his reservations, she is patient with his stumbles and what she calls his tendency towards 'Middle Eastern sugar-coating', throws in some humour about being fired as his mistress, but is gracious, decent, understanding and, above all, kind.

'There aren't many people like you on the earth,' he concludes, and he means it.

What guided him in Berlin was the sudden hope of bypassing some of the shortcomings of his marriage by means of a new but contained foray into someone else's life. But as he perceives it now, such hope could only ever have been sentimental claptrap, and a form of cruelty as well, in which everyone involved would stand to lose and be hurt. There could be no tidy settlement possible in which nothing would be sacrificed. Adventure and security are irreconcilable, he sees. A loving marriage and children kill erotic spontaneity; and an affair kills a marriage. A person cannot be at once a libertine and a married Romantic, however compelling both paradigms might be. He doesn't downplay the loss either way. Saying goodbye to Lauren means safeguarding his marriage but it also means denying himself a critical source of tenderness and elation. Neither the love rat nor the faithful spouse gets it right. There is no solution. He is in tears in the kitchen, sobbing more deeply than he has in years: about what he has lost, what he has endangered and how punishing the choices have been. He has just about enough time to compose himself between the moment the key turns in the lock and Kirsten enters the kitchen.

The weeks that follow will prove a mixture of relief and sadness. His wife will ask him on a couple of occasions if anything is wrong, and the second time, he will make a great effort to adjust his manner so that she won't have to ask him again.

Melancholy isn't, of course, a disorder that needs to be cured. It's a species of intelligent grief which arises when we come face to face with the certainty that disappointment is written into the script from the start.

We have not been singled out. Marrying anyone, even the most suitable of beings, comes down to a case of identifying which variety of suffering we would most like to sacrifice ourselves for.

In an ideal world, marriage vows would be entirely rewritten. At the altar, a couple would speak thus: 'We accept not to panic when, some years from now, what we are doing today will seem like the worst decision of our lives. Yet we promise not to look around, either, for we accept that there cannot be better options out there. Everyone is always impossible. We are a demented species.'

After the solemn repetition of the last sentence by the congregation, the couple would continue: 'We will endeavour to be faithful. At the same time, we are certain that never being allowed to sleep with anyone else is one of the tragedies of existence. We apologize that our jealousies have made this peculiar but sound and non-negotiable restriction very necessary. We promise to make each other the sole repository of our regrets, rather than distribute them through a life of sexual Don Juanism. We have surveyed the different options for unhappiness and it is to each other we have chosen to bind ourselves.'

Spouses who had been cheated on would no longer be at liberty furiously to complain that they had expected their partner to be content with them alone. Instead they could more poignantly and justly cry, 'I was relying on you to be loyal to the specific variety of compromise and unhappiness which our hard-won marriage represents.'

Thereafter, an affair would be a betrayal not of intimate joy, but of a reciprocal pledge to endure the disappointments of marriage with bravery and stoic reserve.

Secrets

No relationship could start without a commitment to wholehearted intimacy. But in order for love to keep going, it also seems impossible to imagine partners not learning to keep a great many of their thoughts to themselves.

We are so impressed by honesty that we forget the virtues of politeness; a desire not always to confront people we care about with the full, hurtful aspects of our nature.

Repression, a degree of restraint and a little dedication to self-editing belong to love just as surely as a capacity for explicit confession. The person who can't tolerate secrets, who in the name of 'being honest' shares information so wounding to the other that it can never be forgotten, this person is no friend of love. And if we suspect (as we should regularly if our relationship is a worthy one) that our partner is also lying (about what she's thinking of, how he judges our work and where she was last night . . .), then we would do well not to act the sharp and relentless inquisitor. It may be kinder, wiser and closer to the true spirit of love to pretend we simply didn't notice.

For Rabih, there is no alternative but to lie for ever about what happened in Berlin. He has to because he knows that telling the truth would beget an even greater order of falsehood: the

profoundly mistaken belief that he no longer loves Kirsten or
else that he is a man who can no longer be trusted in any area of
life. The truth risks distorting the relationship far more than the
untruth.

In the wake of the affair, Rabih adopts a different view of the
purpose of marriage. As a younger man he thought of it as a con-
secration of a special set of feelings: tenderness, desire, enthusiasm,
longing. However, he now understands that it is also, and just as
importantly, an institution, one which is meant to stand fast from
year to year without reference to every passing change in the emotions of its participants. It has its justification in more stable and
enduring phenomena than feelings: in an original act of commitment impervious to later revisions and, more notably, in children,
a class of beings constitutionally uninterested in the daily satisfac-
tions of those who created them.

*For most of recorded history, people stayed married because they were
keen to fit in with the expectations of society, had a few assets to protect
and wanted to maintain the unity of their families. Then, gradually,
another, very different standard took hold: couples were to remain
together, ran the thought, only so long as certain feelings still obtained
between them – feelings of authentic enthusiasm, desire and fulfilment.
In this new Romantic order, spouses could be justified in parting ways
if the marital routine had become deadening, if the children were getting
on their nerves, if sex was no longer enticing or if either party had lately
been feeling a little unhappy.*

The more Rabih appreciates how chaotic and directionless his feelings are, the more sympathetic he grows to the idea of marriage as
an institution. At a conference, he might spy an attractive woman
and want to throw away everything for her sake, only to recognize

two days later that he would prefer to be dead than without Kirsten. Or, during protracted rainy weekends, he might wish that his children would grow up and leave him alone until the end of time so he could read his magazine in peace – and then a day later, at the office, his heart would tighten with grief because a meeting threatened to overrun and get him home an hour too late to put the kids to bed.

Against such a quicksilver backdrop, he recognizes the significance of the art of diplomacy, the discipline of not necessarily always saying what one thinks and not doing what one wants, in the service of greater, more strategic ends.

Rabih keeps in mind the contradictory, sentimental and hormonal forces which constantly pull him in a hundred crazed and inconclusive directions. To honour every one of these would be to annul any chance of leading a coherent life. He knows he will never make progress with the larger projects if he can't stand to be, at least some of the time, inwardly dissatisfied and outwardly inauthentic – if only in relation to such passing sensations as the desire to give away his children or end his marriage over a one-night stand with an American urban planner with exceptionally attractive grey-green eyes.

For Rabih it is assigning too great a weight to his feelings to let them be the lodestars by which his life must always be guided. He is a chaotic chemical proposition in dire need of basic principles to which he can adhere during his brief rational spells. He knows to feel grateful for the fact that his external circumstances will sometimes be out of line with what he experiences in his heart. It is probably a sign that he is on the right track.

BEYOND ROMANTICISM

Attachment Theory

With age, they both feel a new awareness of their own immaturity and, at the same time, a sense that it can hardly be unique to them. There are sure to be others out there who can understand them better than they understand themselves.

They've joked about therapy over the years. At first the jibes were at the discipline's expense: therapy was the exclusive preserve of crazy people with too much time and money on their hands; all therapists were mad themselves; people in trouble should simply talk to their friends more; 'seeing someone' about a problem was what people did in Manhattan, not Lothian. But with every large argument between them, these reassuring clichés have come to seem ever less convincing, and on the day when Rabih furiously knocks over a chair and breaks one of its arms in response to Kirsten's query about a credit card bill, they both know at once, without saying a word, that they need to make an appointment.

It's hard to track down a decent therapist, a good deal harder than locating, for instance, a competent hairdresser, a provider of a service with a perhaps less ambitious claim on humanity's attention. Asking around for recommendations is tricky, because people are prone to interpret the request itself as a sign that the marriage is in trouble – rather than taking it as an indication of its robustness and likely longevity. As with most things that stand properly to help in the course of love, counselling seems gravely unromantic.

They eventually find someone through an online search, a sole practitioner with an office in the centre of town, whose simple website refers to an expertise in 'problems of the couple'. The phrase feels reassuring: their particular issues aren't isolated phenomena, just part of what happens within a well-studied and universally troublesome unit.

The consulting room is three flights up in a gloomy late-nineteenth-century tenement block. But inside it's warm and welcoming, full of books, papers and landscape paintings. The therapist, Mrs Fairbairn, sports a plain, dark-blue smock and a large helmet of tightly curled grey hair that frames a modest and sincere-seeming face. When she sits down in the consulting room, her feet are a significant distance off the floor. Rabih will later ungenerously reflect that the 'hobbit' appears unlikely to have had much first-hand experience of the passions she claims to be an expert on.

Rabih notes a large box of tissues on a little table between him and Kirsten – and feels a surge of protest at its implications. He has no wish to accept the invitation to commit his complex griefs in public to a pile of tissues. As Mrs Fairbairn takes down their phone numbers, he nearly interrupts the proceedings to announce that their coming here was actually a mistake, a rather melodramatic overreaction to a few arguments they have had, and that on second thoughts, the relationship is perfectly fine, and indeed at moments very good. He wants to bolt from the room back out into the normal world, to that café on the corner, where he and Kirsten could have a tuna sandwich and a glass of elderflower cordial and carry on with the ordinary life from which they have so oddly excluded themselves of their own volition from a misplaced sense of inadequacy.

'Let me begin by explaining a few things,' says the therapist in a tightly enunciated, upper-class Edinburgh accent. 'We have fifty minutes, which you will be able to keep track of on the clock above the fireplace. You may be feeling a little apprehensive at this point. It would be unusual if you weren't. You may think either that I know everything about you or that I cannot possibly know anything about you. Neither is exactly true. We are exploring things together. I should add a note of congratulation for your coming here. It requires a bit of bravery, I know. Simply by agreeing to be here, you have taken one of the biggest steps two people can take to try to remain together.'

Behind her is a shelf of key books for her profession: *The Ego and Its Mechanisms of Defence*, *Home Is Where We Start From*, *Separation Anxiety*, *The Echo of Love in Couples' Psychotherapy* and *Self and Other in Object Relations Theory*. She is herself halfway through writing a book, her first, called *Secure and Anxious Attachment in Marital Relationships*, which will be published by a small press in London.

'Tell me, what gave you the idea that you might want to come and see me?' she continues in a more intimate voice.

They met seventeen years ago, explains Kirsten. They have two children. They both lost a parent when they were young. Their lives are busy, fulfilling and, at times, hellish. They have arguments of a kind she hates. Her husband is too often, in her eyes, no longer the man she fell in love with. He gets angry with her, he slams doors. He has called her a cunt.

Mrs Fairbairn looks up from her note-taking with an imperturbable expression which they will come to know well.

All of that is true, admits Rabih, but in Kirsten there is a coldness and occasional silent contempt that he despairs of and that seem designed to make him furious. She responds to worries, his or her own, by falling silent and freezing him out. Often, he questions whether she loves him at all.

Attachment theory, developed by the psychologist John Bowlby and colleagues in England in the 1950s, traces the tensions and conflicts of relationships back to our earliest experience of parental care.

A third of the population of Western Europe and North America is estimated to have experienced some form of early parental disappointment (see C. B. Vassily, 2013), with the result that primitive defence mechanisms have been engaged – in order to ward off fears of intolerable anxiety – and capacities for trust and intimacy have been disrupted. In his great work 'Separation Anxiety' (1959), Bowlby argues that those who have been let down by the early family environment will generally develop two kinds of responses when they grow up and face difficulties or ambiguities in relationships: first, a tendency towards fearful, clinging and controlling behaviour – the pattern Bowlby calls 'anxious attachment' – and second, an inclination towards a defensive retreating manoeuvre, which he calls 'avoidant attachment'. The anxious person is prone to check up on their partner constantly, to have explosions of jealousy and to spend a lot of their lives regretting that their relationships are not 'closer'. The avoidant person for their part will speak of a need for 'space', they'll enjoy their own company and will find requirements for sexual intimacy daunting at points.

Up to 70 per cent of patients seeking couples' therapy will exhibit either the anxious or the avoidant mode of behaviour. Very frequently, couples will contain one avoidant partner and

one anxious one, with each set of responses aggravating the
other in a spiral of declining trust.

Dr Joanna Fairbairn, *Secure and Anxious Attachment in
Marital Relationships: An Object Relations View*
(Karnac Books, London, forthcoming)

It is humbling to accept that they aren't going to understand one
another spontaneously. To be here means that they have given up
intuiting what might be happening inside their so-called soulmate.
The Romantic dreams are being surrendered, to be replaced – over
many months – by minute examinations of some ostensibly minor
moments of domestic life, though there are no such things as minor
moments in Mrs Fairbairn's eyes; an unkind remark, a transient
impatience and a wounding brusqueness are the raw materials of
her trade.

Mrs Fairbairn is helping to defuse bombs. It might seem silly,
to spend fifty minutes (and £75) on how Rabih responded when
Kirsten called upstairs to him for the second time to make his way
down to lay the table or Kirsten's way of reacting to Esther's
disappointing geography results . . . But these are the breeding
grounds for issues that, if left unchecked, could develop into the
sort of catastrophes that society is more prepared to focus its attention on: domestic violence, family break-ups, the interventions of
social services, court orders . . . Everything begins with small
humiliations and let-downs.

Today Rabih brings up an argument from the night before. It
was about work and money: there is a danger that his firm will
have to freeze or reduce salaries in the near term, which could cause
them to fall behind on mortgage payments. Kirsten appeared
almost indifferent. Why, when faced with something so serious,
does his wife always respond in such unreassuring ways? Couldn't

she have found something, anything, helpful to say? Did she even hear properly? Why does she so often answer him with a puzzling 'Hmm' just when he most needs her support? That's why he shouted at her, swore, then stalked off. It wasn't ideal, but she was seriously letting him down.

> A sign of an anxiously attached person is an intolerance of, and dramatic reaction to, ambiguous situations – like a silence, a delay or a non-committal remark. These are quickly interpreted in negative ways, as insults or malevolent attacks. For the anxiously attached, any minor slight, hasty word or oversight can be experienced as an intense threat, looming as a harbinger of the break-up of a relationship. More objective explanations slip out of reach. Inside, anxiously attached people often feel as if they were fighting for their lives – though they are typically unable to explain their fragility to those around them, who, understandably, may instead label them as cantankerous, irritable or cruel.

What a silly thing to say, protests Kirsten. He's exaggerating again, as he tends to do about so many things, from how hard it's raining to how terrible some meal at a restaurant is – like that time they went to Portugal and all he could talk about for months afterwards was what a fleapit the hotel had been, as if that was the end of the world, even when the children thought it was fine.

Her response, she adds, certainly didn't justify his sort of reaction. Was it worth storming out of the room for? What kind of adult has such a temper? She holds out an implicit invitation for Mrs Fairbairn to endorse her as the reasonable one in the couple and, as a fellow woman, to join her in marvelling at the folly and melodrama of men.

But Mrs Fairbairn doesn't like being pressed to take sides. This is part of her genius. She doesn't care for anyone being 'in the right'. She wants to sort out what each side is feeling, and then make sure the other side hears it sympathetically.

'What do you feel about Kirsten at times like that, when she doesn't say very much?' she asks Rabih.

It's an absurd question, he thinks; last night's irritation begins to revive in him.

'I feel exactly as you would expect, that she's horrible.'

' "Horrible"? Just because I don't say precisely what you want to hear, I'm horrible?' interjects Kirsten.

'A minute, please, Kirsten,' cautions Mrs Fairbairn. 'I want to explore for a little longer what Rabih experiences at such moments. What is it like for you when you think Kirsten has let you down?'

Rabih applies no further rational brake, letting his unconscious speak for once: 'Scared. Abandoned. Helpless.'

There is silence now, as there often is after one of them says something significant.

'I feel I'm alone. That I don't matter. That she doesn't give a damn about me.'

He stops. There are – rather unexpectedly, perhaps – tears welling up in his eyes.

'It sounds difficult,' says Mrs Fairbairn, in a neutral and yet engaged way.

'He doesn't sound scared to *me*,' Kirsten observes. 'A man who screams and swears at his wife hardly seems a prime candidate to be thought of as a poor scared lambie.'

But Mrs Fairbairn has the problem caught firmly in her therapeutic tweezers and she isn't going to let it go. It is a pattern: over some matter where he needs reassurance, Rabih experiences Kirsten as withdrawn and cold. He gets scared, loses his temper and then finds Kirsten even more withdrawn. The fear and the anger increase, as does the distance. Kirsten sees him as arrogant and a bully. Her history has taught her that men have a proclivity for overbearing behaviour – and that it is a woman's role to resist it through strength and formality. Forgiveness at this point is not on the cards. But inside Rabih there is no strength at all, he is simply flailing, at his wits' end, weak and humiliated by signs of her apparent indifference. It is therefore unfortunate, bordering on the tragic, that his way of responding to his vulnerabilities takes a form that masks them entirely and seems guaranteed to alienate the person he wants so badly to be comforted by.

But now, once a week, on a Wednesday at midday, there is a chance to interrupt the vicious circle. With Mrs Fairbairn protecting Kirsten from Rabih's annoyance and Rabih from Kirsten's aloofness, each spouse is invited to peer beneath the hurtful surface of the other, to see the pitiful frightened child within.

'Kirsten, do you think shouting, and sometimes swearing, are the actions of a man who feels strong?' Mrs Fairbairn ventures in one of her few more directive moments, when she feels an insight is within the reach of her clients.

She knows how to step very lightly. The books on the shelf may have rather heavy-footed titles but in the flow of a session the diminutive therapist moves like a ballerina.

The difficult dynamic between the couple extends to sex. When Kirsten is tired or distracted, Rabih quickly, far too quickly, falls into despondency. His mind holds fast to a powerful narrative about his own repulsiveness. This sense of self-disgust, which long pre-dated Kirsten, has as one of its central features an inability to be explained to others, even though it ushers in a stance of bitterness with those who evoke it. An unconsummated evening will thus generally end up as the disguised spur to sarcastic or wounding remarks made by Rabih the next day – which will then fuel greater (and equally unspoken) efforts on Kirsten's part to step back. After a few days of being shut out, Rabih will get fed up and accuse Kirsten of being cold and weird – to which she will reply that she suspects he must really enjoy upsetting her, since he does it so often. She retreats to a sad but oddly comforting and familiar place inside her head where she hides when others let her down (as they tend to do) and takes comfort in books and music. She is an expert in self-protection and defence; she has been in training for much of her life.

> An avoidant attachment style is marked by a strong desire to avoid conflict and to reduce exposure to the other when emotional needs have not been met. The avoidant person quickly presumes that others are keen to attack them and that they cannot be reasoned with. One just has to escape, pull up the drawbridge and go cold. Regrettably, the avoidant party cannot normally explain their fearful and defensive pattern to their partner, so that the reasons behind their distant and absent behaviour remain clouded and are easy to mistake for being uncaring and unengaged, when in fact the opposite is true: the avoidant party cares very deeply indeed, it is just that loving has come to feel far too risky.

While never forcing conclusions, Mrs Fairbairn nonetheless holds up a figurative mirror so that Kirsten can start to see the impact she has on others. She helps her become aware of her tendency to flee and to respond to stress through silence, and encourages her to consider how these strategies might affect those who depend upon her. Much like Rabih, Kirsten has a habit of expressing her disappointments in such a way that they are guaranteed not to draw sympathy from those whose love she needs most urgently.

Rabih never brings up his night with Lauren directly. He sees that the priority is to understand why it happened rather than to confess that it did, in a way that might unleash the sorts of insecurities that would destroy trust between Kirsten and himself for ever. He wonders, between sessions with Mrs Fairbairn, what could have rendered him so apparently blithe and indifferent about hurting his wife and sees that there could really only have been one explanation: that he must have felt so hurt by things in the relationship that he had reached a point of not caring too much that he might severely wound Kirsten. He slept with Lauren not out of desire, but out of anger, the sort of anger that doesn't admit to its own existence, a sullen, repressed, proud fury. Explaining to Kirsten, in a way she can understand, that he has felt let down will be central to saving his marriage.

At the heart of their struggles, there is an issue of trust – a virtue which comes easily to neither of them. They are wounded creatures who had to cope with undue disappointments as children and have consequently grown into powerfully defended adults, awkward about all emotional undress. They are experts in attack strategy and fortress construction; what they are rather less good at, like fighters adjusting badly to civilian life after an armistice, is tolerating the anxieties that come with letting down their guard and admitting to their own fragilities and sorrows.

Rabih anxiously attacks; Kirsten avoidantly withdraws. They are two people who need one another badly and yet are simultaneously terrified of letting on just how much they do so. Neither stays with an injury long enough truly to acknowledge or feel it, or to explain it to the person who inflicted it. It takes reserves of confidence they don't possess to keep faith with the one who has offended them. They would need to trust the other sufficiently to make it clear that they aren't really 'angry' or 'cold' but are instead, and always, something far more basic, touching and deserving of affection: hurt. They cannot offer each other that most romantically necessary of gifts: a guide to their own vulnerabilities.

A questionnaire originally devised by Hazan and Shaver (1987) has been widely used to measure attachment styles. To ascertain what type they might be, respondents are asked to report which of the following three statements they can most closely relate to:

1. 'I want emotionally close relationships, but I find that other people are often disappointing or mean without good reason. I worry that I will be hurt if I allow myself to become too close to others. I don't mind spending time on my own.' (Avoidant Attachment)

2. 'I want to be emotionally intimate with others, but I often find that they are reluctant to get as close as I would like. I worry that others don't value me as much as I value them. It can make me feel very upset and annoyed.' (Anxious Attachment)

3. 'It is relatively easy for me to become emotionally close to others. I feel comfortable depending on others and having them depend on me. I don't worry about being alone or not being accepted by others.' (Secure Attachment)

The labels themselves certainly lack glamour. It's rather a blow to the ego to be forced to conceive of oneself not as some kind of infinitely nuanced character whom a novelist might struggle to capture in eight hundred pages, but rather as a generic type who could easily fit within the parameters of a few paragraphs in a psychoanalytic textbook. The terms 'avoidant' and 'anxious' are hardly typical in a love story, but if 'Romantic' is taken to mean 'helpful to the progress of love', then they turn out to be among the most romantic words Kirsten and Rabih will ever stumble upon, for they enable them to grasp patterns that have been destructively at work between them every day of their married lives.

They come to appreciate the unusual psychotherapeutic diplomatic back-channel which has made a new mode of discourse
possible for them, a sanctuary where weekly they can confess to
being furious or sad under the benevolent watch of a referee who
is guaranteed to contain the other's reaction long enough to secure
a necessary degree of understanding and perhaps empathy. Thou-
sands of years of halting steps towards civilization have at last led to
a forum where two people can painstakingly discuss how hurtful
one of them has been to the other about laying a table or saying
something at a party or arranging a holiday, with neither side being
permitted simply to get up, storm out or swear. Therapy is, Kirsten
and Rabih conclude, in some ways, the greatest invention of the age.

The conversations they have in Mrs Fairbairn's presence start
to colour how they talk to one another at home. They begin to
internalize the therapist's benign, judicious voice. 'What would
Joanna (a name they never use in her presence) say?' becomes a
ritual, playful question between them – much as Catholics might
once have tried to imagine Jesus's response to a trial of life.

'If you carry on getting annoyed with me, I'm going to end up
avoidant,' Kirsten might warn in response to a stand-off with
Rabih.

They still joke about therapy, just no longer at its expense.

It is a pity, therefore, that the insights on offer in the consulting
room are so negligible in the wider culture. Their conversations
feel like a small laboratory of maturity in a world besotted by the
idea of love as an instinct and a feeling beyond examination. That
Mrs Fairbairn's room is tucked up some tenement stairs seems symbolic of the marginalized nature of her occupation. She is the
champion of a truth that Rabih and Kirsten are now intimate with,
but which they know is woefully prone to get lost in the surrounding noise: that love is a skill, not just an enthusiasm.

Maturity

Throughout the winter Rabih works on designs for a gymnasium. He meets a dozen times with the members of the local education authority who are commissioning it. It promises to be an exceptional building, with a system of skylights which will make it bright inside even on the dullest days. Professionally speaking, it may be the beginning of something very substantial for him. And then, in the spring, they call him back in and, in that aggressive manner sometimes adopted by people who feel so guilty about letting someone down that they become offensive, bluntly tell him it's off – and that they've decided to go with another practice with more experience. That's when the not-sleeping begins.

Insomnia can, when it goes on for weeks, be hell. But in smaller doses – a night here and there – it doesn't always need a cure. It may even be an asset, a help with some key troubles of the soul. Crucial insights that we need to convey to ourselves can often be received only at night, like city church bells that have to wait until dark to be heard.

During the day he has to be dutiful towards others. Alone in the den, past midnight, he can return to a bigger, more private duty. His thought processes would no doubt sound weird to Kirsten,

Esther and William. They need him to be a certain way, and he doesn't want to let them down or scare them with the strangeness of his perceptions; they have a right to benefit from his predictability. But there are now other inner demands on his attention. Insomnia is his mind's revenge for all the tricky thoughts he has carefully avoided during the daylight hours.

Ordinary life rewards a practical, unintrospective outlook. There's too little time and too much fear for anything else. We let ourselves be guided by an instinct for self-preservation: we push ourselves forward, strike back when we're hit, turn the blame on to others, quell stray questions and cleave closely to a flattering image of where we're headed. We have little option but to be relentlessly on our own side.

Only at those rare moments when the stars are out and nothing further will be needed from us until dawn can we loosen our hold on our ego for the sake of a more honest and less parochial perspective.

He looks at the familiar facts in a new way: he is a coward, a dreamer, an unfaithful husband and an overly possessive, clingy father. His life is held together by string. He is over halfway through his career and he has achieved next to nothing in comparison with the hopes that were once placed on him.

He can, at three a.m., be oddly unsentimental in listing his faults: a wilful streak that provokes distrust in his superiors, a tendency to get offended too easily, a preference for caution based on a terror of rejection. He has not had the self-confidence to stick with things. By his age, others have gone ahead and set up their own architectural practices, instead of waiting to be asked and then blaming the world for not begging hard enough. There is precisely one building – a data-storage facility in Hertfordshire – with his name on it. He is on track to die with the largest part of his talents still unexploited, registering as mere flashes of inspiration that he occasionally perceives out of the corner of his mind's eye while he's in the shower or driving alone down the motorway.

At this point, he is beyond self-pity, the shallow belief that what has happened to him is rare or undeserved. He has lost faith in his own innocence and uniqueness. This isn't a midlife crisis; it's more that he is finally, some thirty years too late, leaving adolescence behind.

He sees he is a man with an exaggerated longing for Romantic love who nevertheless understands little about kindness and even less about communication. He is someone afraid of openly striving for happiness who takes shelter in a stance of pre-emptive disappointment and cynicism.

So this is what it is to be a failure. The chief characteristic may be silence: the phone doesn't ring, he isn't asked out, nothing new happens. For most of his adult life he has conceived of failure in the form of a spectacular catastrophe, only to recognize, at last, that it has in fact crept up on him imperceptibly, through cowardly inaction.

Yet, surprisingly, it's OK. One gets used to everything, even humiliation. The apparently unendurable has a habit of coming to seem, eventually, not so bad.

He has already sucked too much of life's bounty, without particular profit and to no good effect. He has been on the earth for too many decades; he has never had to till the soil or go to bed hungry, yet he has left his privileges largely untouched, like a spoilt child.

His dreams were once very grand indeed: he would be another Louis Kahn or Le Corbusier, Mies van der Rohe or Geoffrey Bawa. He was going to bring a new kind of architecture into being: locally specific, elegant, harmonious, technologically cutting-edge, progressive.

Instead he is the almost-broke deputy director of a second-rate urban design firm, with a single building – more of a shed, really – to his name.

Nature embeds in us insistent dreams of success. For the species, there must be an evolutionary advantage in being hard-wired for such striving; restlessness has given us cities, libraries, spaceships.

But this impulse doesn't leave much opportunity for individual equilibrium. The price of a few works of genius throughout history is a substantial portion of the human race being daily sickened by anxiety and disappointment.

Rabih used to assume that only the flawless version of anything was worth having. He was a perfectionist. If the car was scratched, he couldn't enjoy driving it; if the room was untidy, he couldn't rest; if his lover didn't understand parts of him, the entire relationship was a charade. Now 'good enough' is becoming good enough.

He notes a developing interest in certain sorts of news stories about middle-aged men. There was a guy from Glasgow who threw himself under a train, having amassed large debts and been caught out in an affair by his wife. Another drove his car into the sea near Aberdeen following some online scandal. It doesn't, in the end, take very much, Rabih can see: just a few mistakes and suddenly one is in the realm of catastrophe. With a few twists of the dial, with enough outside pressure, he, too, would be capable of anything. What enables him to think of himself as sane is only a certain fragile chemical good fortune, but he knows he would be very much in the market for a tragedy if ever life chose to test him properly.

At those times when he is neither fully awake nor quite asleep but travelling through the interstitial zones of consciousness, at two or three a.m., he feels how many images and stray memories his mind holds, all waiting to come to his attention when the rest of the static has receded: glimpses of a trip to Bangkok eight years before, the surreal view of villages in India after a night squashed against an aeroplane window; the cold tiled bathroom floor in the house his family lived in in Athens; the first snowfall he ever experienced, on a holiday in eastern Switzerland; the low grey sky observed on a walk across fields in Norfolk; a corridor leading towards a swimming pool at university; the night spent with Esther in hospital when they operated on her finger . . . The logic of some things may fade, but none of the images ever really goes away.

During his sleepless nights, he occasionally thinks about and misses his mother. He wishes with embarrassing intensity that he might be eight again and curled up under a blanket, with a slight fever, and that she could bring him food and read to him. He longs for her to reassure him about the future, absolve him of his sins and comb his hair neatly into a left-sided parting. He is at least mature enough to know there is something important which ought to resist immediate censorship in these regressive states. He can see that he hasn't, despite the outward signs, come very far.

He realizes that anxiety will always dog him. It may appear that each new wave of it is about this or that particular thing – the party where he won't know many people, the complicated journey he has to make to an unfamiliar country, a dilemma at work – but considered from a broader perspective, the problem is always larger, more damning and more fundamental.

He once fantasized that his worries would be stilled if he lived elsewhere, if he attained a few professional goals, if he had a family. But nothing has ever made a difference. He is, he can see, anxious to the core, in his most basic make-up: a frightened, ill-adjusted creature.

There is a photograph he loves in the kitchen, of Kirsten, William, Esther and himself in a park on an autumn day, throwing leaves at one another from a pile blown together by the wind. Joy and abandon are evident in all their faces, a delight in being able to make a mess without consequence. But he recalls, also, how inwardly troubled he was on that day; there was something at work with an engineering company, he was keen to get home and make some calls to an English client, his credit card was far above its limit. Only when events are over is there really any chance for Rabih to enjoy them.

He is aware that his strong, capable wife is not the best person around whom to have a nervous breakdown. There was a time when he would have felt bitter about this. 'Insomnia isn't glamorous. Just come to bed,' is all Kirsten would say if she woke up now and saw the light on in the den. He's learned, over many painful episodes, that his beautiful, intelligent wife doesn't *do* reassurance.

But better than that, he's started to understand why. She isn't mean; it's her experience of men and her defences against being let down kicking in. It's just how she processes challenges. It helps to see these things; he is accruing alternatives to vengeance and anger.

Few in this world are ever simply nasty; those who hurt us are themselves in pain. The appropriate response is hence never cynicism or aggression but, at the rare moments one can manage it, always love.

Kirsten's mother is in hospital. She has been there for two weeks. It started off as something innocuous having to do with her kidneys; now the prognosis is suddenly far graver. Normally so strong, Kirsten is ashen and lost.

They went up to see her on Sunday. She was extremely frail and spoke softly and only to make simple requests: a glass of water, the lamp tilted so there would be a little less light in her eyes. At one point she took Rabih's hand in hers and gave him a smile. 'Look after her, will you?' she said, and then, with the old sharpness, 'If she lets you.' A forgiveness, of sorts.

He knows that he never found favour in Mrs McLelland's eyes. At first he resented it; now, as a parent himself, he can sympathize. He isn't looking forward to Esther's husband, either. How could a parent ever truly approve? How could they possibly be expected, after eighteen or so years of answering to a child's every need, to react enthusiastically to a new and competing source of love? How could anyone sincerely perform the requisite emotional somersault and not suspect in their heart (and let on as much, through a succession of more or less sour remarks) that their child had mistakenly fallen into the clutches of someone fundamentally unsuited to the complex and unique task of administering to them?

Kirsten cries uncontrollably after their first visit to Raigmore Hospital. Back home, she sends the children to play with their friends; she can't be a parent (the one who tries never to frighten others by revealing their pain) right now, she needs to be a child again for a while. She can't overcome the horror of her mother looking sallow and emaciated against the institutional blue sheets. How could this be happening? She is at some level still deeply attached to her impression, formed in her fifth or sixth year, of her mother as someone strong, capable and in charge. Kirsten was the little one who could be scooped up into the air and told what needed to happen next. She craved this authority in the years after her father left. The two McLelland women knew how to stick together;

they were a team, involved in the best kind of sedition. Now Kirsten is in the corridor at Raigmore again, quizzing an alarmingly young doctor about how many months there will be left. The world has been upended.

We start off in childhood believing parents might have access to a superior kind of knowledge and experience. They look, for a while, astonishingly competent. Our exaggerated esteem is touching, but also intensely prob-lematic, for it sets them up as the ultimate objects of blame when we gradually discover that they are flawed, sometimes unkind, in areas ignorant and utterly unable to save us from certain troubles. It can take a while, until the fourth decade or the final hospital scenes, for a more forgiving stance to emerge. Their new condition, frail and frightened, reveals in a compellingly physical way something which has always been true psychologically: that they are uncertain vulnerable creatures motiv-ated more by anxiety, fear, a clumsy love and unconscious compulsions than by godlike wisdom and moral clarity – and cannot, therefore, forever be held responsible for either their own shortcomings or our many disappointments.

In those moods when Rabih can at long last break free of his ego, it isn't just one or two people he feels he can forgive more easily. It may even be, at an extreme, that no human being any longer lies outside the circle of his sympathy.

He sees goodness in unexpected places. He is moved by the benevolence of the office administrator, a widow in her mid-fifties whose son has just gone off to university in Leeds. She is cheerful and strong, an extraordinary accomplishment which she extends over every hour of every working day. She takes care to ask all the staff how they are. She remembers birthdays and fills in idle min-utes with reflections that are always encouraging and tender. As a younger man he wouldn't have taken any notice of such a minor demonstration of grace, but by now he has been humbled enough by life to know to stoop down and pick up the smaller blessings wherever they come. He has, without trying and without pride, become a little nicer.

He is readier to be generous, too, from a sense of how much he needs the charity of others. When others are vindictive, he is more interested in mitigating circumstances, and in any bits of the truth that cast a less moralistic light on viciousness and bad behaviour. Cynicism is too easy, and it gets you nowhere.

He becomes aware, for the first time in his life, of the beauty of flowers. He remembers harbouring a near-hatred of them as an adolescent. It seemed absurd that anyone should take joy in something so small and so temporary when there were surely greater, more permanent things on which to pin ambitions. He himself wanted glory and intensity. To be detained by a flower was a symbol of a dangerous resignation. Now he is beginning to get the point. The love of flowers is a consequence of modesty and an accommodation with disappointment. Some things need to go permanently wrong before we can start to admire the stem of a rose or the petals of a bluebell. But once we realize that the larger dreams are always compromised in some way, with what gratitude we may turn to these minuscule islands of serene perfection and delight.

Held up against certain ideals of success, his life has been a deep disappointment. But he can also see that it is, in the end, no great achievement simply to fixate on failure. There is valour in being able to identify a forgiving, hopeful perspective on one's life, in knowing how to be a friend to oneself, because one has a responsibility to others to endure.

Sometimes he has a hot bath in the middle of the night and takes stock of his body under the bright light. Ageing is a bit like looking tired, but in a way that no amount of sleep will repair. Every year it will get a little worse. Today's so-called bad photograph will be next year's good one. Nature's kind trick is to make everything happen so slowly that we don't get as scared as we should. One day his hands will be liver-spotted, like those of the elderly uncles he knew in his childhood. Everything that has happened to others will happen to him, too. No one gets away.

He is a collection of tissues and cells delicately and intricately conjoined and brought to life for only an instant. It will take just one sharp collision or a fall to render them inanimate again. All the seriousness of his plans depends on a steady flow of blood to his brain through a vulnerable network of capillaries. Should any of these suffer even the tiniest of failures, the tenuous sense he has begun to make of life will at once be erased. He is just a fortuitous constellation of atoms which have chosen to resist entropy for a few moments within cosmic eternity. He wonders which of his organs will fail first.

He is only a visitor who has managed to confuse his self with the world. He had assumed he was yet another stable object, like the city of Edinburgh or a tree or a book, whereas he is more like a shadow or a sound.

Death will be nothing too bad, he supposes: the constituent parts of him will be redistributed and returned. Life has been long already and it will, at a point whose outlines he now intuits, soon be time to release and give others a go.

One evening, returning home through the dark streets, he spots a florist's shop. He must have passed it many, many times, and yet he's never taken any notice of it before. The front window is brightly illuminated and filled with a variety of blooms. He steps in and an elderly woman smiles warmly at him. His eye is drawn to the first native flowers of a tentative spring: snowdrops. He watches the woman's hands wrap the little bunch in fine white tissue.

'For someone nice, I think?' She smiles at him.

'My wife,' he replies.

'Lucky woman,' she says as she hands him the flowers and his change. He hopes to get home and, on this occasion, prove the florist right.

Ready for Marriage

They have been married for sixteen years and yet only now, a little late, does Rabih feel ready for marriage. It's not the paradox it seems. Given that marriage yields its important lessons only to those who have signed up for its curriculum, it's normal that readiness should tend to follow rather than precede the ceremony itself – perhaps by a decade or two.

Rabih recognizes that it's a mere sleight of language that allows him to maintain that he has been married only once. What has conveniently looked like a single relationship in fact sits across so many evolutions, disconnections, renegotiations, intervals of distance and emotional homecomings that he has in truth gone through at least a dozen divorces and remarriages – just to the same person.

He is on a long drive down to Manchester for a client meeting. This is where he can think best, very early in the morning, in the car, with the roads almost entirely clear and no one to talk to but himself.

Once, you were deemed ready for matrimony when you'd reached certain financial and social milestones: when you had a home to your name, a trousseau full of linen, a set of qualifications on the mantelpiece or a few cows and a parcel of land in your possession.

Then, under the influence of Romantic ideology, such practicalities grew to seem altogether too mercenary and calculating, and the focus shifted to emotional qualities. It came to be thought important to have the right feelings; among these, a sense of having hit upon a soulmate, a faith in being perfectly understood, a certainty of never wanting to sleep with anyone else again.

The Romantic ideas are, he knows now, a recipe for disaster. His readiness for marriage is based on a quite different set of criteria. He is ready for marriage because – to begin the list – he has given up on perfection.

Pronouncing a lover 'perfect' can only be a sign that we have failed to understand them. We can claim to have begun to know someone only when they have substantially disappointed us.

However, the problems aren't theirs alone. Whoever we could meet would be radically imperfect: the stranger on the train, the old school acquaintance, the new friend online . . . Each of these, too, would be guaranteed to let us down. The facts of life have deformed all of our natures. No one among us has come through unscathed. We were all (necessarily) less than ideally parented. We fight rather than explain, we nag rather than teach, we fret instead of analysing our worries, we lie and scatter blame where it doesn't belong.

The chances of a perfect human emerging from the perilous gauntlet are non-existent. We don't have to know a stranger very well before knowing this about them. Their particular way of being maddening won't be immediately apparent (it could take as long as a couple of years), but its existence can be theoretically assumed from the start.

Choosing a person to marry is hence just a matter of deciding exactly what kind of suffering we want to endure, rather than of imagining we have found a way to skirt round the rules of emotional existence. We will all by definition end up with that stock character of our nightmares, 'the wrong person'.

This needn't be a disaster, however. Enlightened Romantic pessimism simply assumes that one person can't be everything to another. We should look for ways to accommodate ourselves as gently and as kindly as we can to the awkward realities of living alongside another fallen creature. There can only ever be a 'good enough' marriage.

For this realization to sink in, it helps to have had a few lovers before settling down, not in order to have had a chance to locate 'the right person', but in order to have had an ample opportunity to discover at first hand, and in many different contexts, the truth that there isn't any such person; and that everyone really is a bit wrong when considered from close up.

Rabih feels ready for marriage because he has despaired of being fully understood.

Love begins with the experience of being understood in highly supportive and uncommon ways. They grasp the lonely parts of us; we don't have to explain why we find a particular joke so funny; we hate the same people; we both want to try that rather specialized sexual scenario.

It cannot continue. When we run up against the reasonable limits of our lovers' capacities for understanding, we mustn't blame them for dereliction. They were not tragically inept. They couldn't fully fathom who we were — and we could do no better. Which is normal. No one properly gets, or can fully sympathize with, anyone else.

Rabih feels ready for marriage because he realizes he is crazy.

It's profoundly counter-intuitive for us to think of ourselves as mad. We seem so normal and mostly so good — to ourselves. It's everyone else who *is out of step . . . And yet maturity begins with the capacity to sense and, in good time and without defensiveness, admit to our own craziness. If we are not regularly deeply embarrassed by who we are, the journey to self-knowledge hasn't begun.*

Rabih is ready for marriage because he has understood that it isn't Kirsten who is difficult.

They seem 'difficult', of course, within the cage of marriage; when they lose their tempers over such petty things: logistics, in-laws, cleaning rotas, parties, the groceries . . . But it's not the other person's fault, it's what we're trying to do with them. It's the institution of marriage that is principally impossible, not the individuals involved.

Rabih is ready for marriage because he is prepared to love rather than be loved.

We speak of 'love' as if it were a single, undifferentiated thing, but it comprises two very different modes: being loved and loving. We should marry when we are ready to do the latter and have become aware of our unnatural and dangerous fixation on the former.

We start out knowing only about 'being loved'. It comes to seem — quite wrongly — the norm. To the child, it feels as if the parent were just spontaneously on hand to comfort, guide, entertain, feed and clear up, while remaining almost constantly warm and cheerful.

We take this idea of love with us into adulthood. Grown up, we hope for a re-creation of what it felt like to be ministered to and indulged. In a secret corner of our mind, we picture a lover who will anticipate our needs, read our hearts, act selflessly and make everything better. It sounds 'romantic'; yet it is a blueprint for disaster.

Rabih is ready for marriage because he understands that sex will always cohabit uneasily with love.

The Romantic view expects that love and sex will be aligned. We are properly ready for marriage when we are strong enough to embrace a life of frustration.

We must concede that adultery cannot be a workable answer, for no one can be its victim and not feel forever cut to the core. A single mean- ingless adventure truly does have a recurring habit of ending everything. It's impossible for the victims of adultery to appreciate what might actu- ally have been going through a partner's mind during the 'betrayal', when they lay entwined with a stranger for a few hours. We can hear their defence as often as we like, but we'll be sure of one thing in our hearts: that they were hell-bent on humiliating us and that every ounce of their love has evaporated, along with their status as trustworthy humans. To insist on any other conclusion is like arguing against the tide.

He is ready for marriage because (on a good day) he is happy to be taught and calm about teaching.

We are ready for marriage when we accept that in a number of significant areas our partner will be wiser, more reasonable and more mature than we are. We should want to learn from them. We should bear having things pointed out to us. And at other moments we should be ready to model ourselves on the best pedagogues and deliver our suggestions with- out shouting or expecting the other simply to know. Only if we were already perfect could the idea of mutual education be dismissed as unloving.

Rabih and Kirsten are ready to be married because they are aware, deep down, that they are not compatible.

The Romantic vision of marriage stresses the importance of finding the 'right' person, which is taken to mean someone in sympathy with the raft of our interests and values. There is no such person over the long term. We are too varied and peculiar. There cannot be lasting congruence. The partner truly best suited to us is not the one who miraculously happens to share every taste, but the one who can negotiate differences in taste with intelligence and good grace.

Rather than some notional idea of perfect complementarity, it is the capacity to tolerate dissimilarity that is the true marker of the 'right' person. Compatibility is an achievement of love; it shouldn't be its precondition.

Rabih is ready for marriage because he is fed up with most love stories; and because the versions of love presented in films and novels so seldom match what he now knows from lived experience.

By the standards of most love stories, our own, real relationships are almost all damaged and unsatisfactory. No wonder separation and divorce so often appear inevitable. But we should be careful not to judge our relationships by the expectations imposed on us by a frequently misleading aesthetic medium. The fault lies with art, not life. Rather than split up, we may need to tell ourselves more accurate stories — stories that don't dwell so much on the beginning, that don't promise us complete understanding, that strive to normalize our troubles and show us a melancholy yet hopeful path through the course of love.

The Future

It is Kirsten's birthday and Rabih has arranged for them to spend the night at a wildly luxurious and expensive hotel in the Highlands. They drop the children off with a cousin of hers in Fort William and drive to the nineteenth-century castle. It promises battlements, five stars, room service, a billiard room, a pool, a French restaurant and a ghost.

The children have made their unhappiness clear. Esther has accused her father of ruining her mother's birthday. 'I just know you're going to get bored without us and that Mummy is going to miss us,' she insists. 'I don't think you should be away for so long' (they will be meeting again the following afternoon). William reassures his sister that their parents can always watch television and might even find a games room with a computer.

Their room is in a turret at the top of the building. There is a large bathtub in the centre and the windows look out over a succession of peaks dominated by Ben Nevis, which is still carrying a light dusting of snow on its tip in June.

Once the young bellboy has dropped off their luggage, they feel awkward in each other's presence. It has been years, many years, since they have been alone in a hotel room together, without children or anything in particular to do over the next twenty-four hours.

It feels as if they are having an affair, so differently do they act towards each other in this setting. Encouraged by the dignity and quiet of the vast, high-ceilinged room, they are more formal and respectful. Kirsten asks Rabih with unaccustomed solicitude what he might like to order from the room-service tea menu – and he runs her a bath.

The trick is perhaps not to start a new life but to learn to reconsider the old one with less jaded and habituated eyes.

He lies on the bed and watches her soak in the tub: her hair is up and she is reading a magazine. He feels sorry for and guilty about the troubles they have caused each other. He looks at a set of brochures he has picked up off the desk. There is shooting offered in September and options for salmon fishing in February. When she is finished, she rises from the bath with her arms crossed over her breasts. He is touched, and a little aroused, by her reserve.

They go downstairs for dinner. The restaurant is candlelit, with high-backed chairs and antlers hanging on the walls. The head waiter describes the six-course menu in an absurdly high-flown manner which they nonetheless surprise themselves by very much enjoying. They know enough about the squalor of domesticity, by now, not to resist the chance to revel in a bit of elaborately staged hospitality.

They start by talking about the children, their friends and work, and then, after the third course – venison on a bed of celeriac mousse – they move on to less familiar territory, discussing her suppressed ambition to take up an instrument again and his desire to invite her to Beirut. Kirsten even begins, finally, to speak of her father. She explains that whenever she's in a new place, she wonders whether he might happen to be living somewhere nearby. She wants to try to get in touch with him. Her eyes shine with withheld tears, and she says she's tired of being angry with him her whole life long. Maybe she would have done the same thing as he did, in his shoes. Almost. She'd like him to meet his grandchildren and (she adds with a smile) her horrible and peculiar Middle Eastern husband.

Rabih has ordered some recklessly expensive French wine, almost the price of the room itself, and it has begun to have its effect. He wants to get another bottle, for the hell of it. He senses the psychological and moral role of wine, its capacity to open up channels of feeling and communication which are otherwise closed off – not merely to offer a crude escape from difficulties, but to allow access to emotions which daily life unfairly leaves no room for. Getting very drunk hasn't seemed so important in a long time.

He realizes there is still so much he doesn't know about his wife. She seems almost a stranger to him. He imagines that it's their first date and she has agreed to come and fuck him in a Scottish castle. She has left behind her children and her awful husband. She is touching him under the table, looking at him with her clever, sceptical eyes and spilling a bit of her wine on the tablecloth.

He's very grateful to the waiters in their black uniforms and the locally reared lamb that has died for them and the three-layer fondant chocolate cake and the petits fours and the chamomile tea for conspiring to create a setting which places the fundamental mystery and charm of his wife on appropriate display.

She isn't good at receiving compliments, of course, but Rabih knows this by now, knows where it all comes from, the independence and reticence which have been so upsetting to him in the past but won't be so much in the future, and he ploughs on nevertheless and tells her how beautiful she looks, what wise eyes she has, how proud he is of her and how sorry he is about everything. And instead of rebuffing his words with one of her normal stoic remarks, she smiles – a warm wide quiet smile – and says thank you and squeezes his hand and may even be starting to tear up slightly again, just as the waiter comes and asks if he can get Madam anything else at all. She replies, slurring slightly, 'Just some more loveliness', then catches herself.

It's gone to her head too, making her brave; brave enough to be weak. It feels like a dam breaking inside her. She has had enough of resisting him; she wants to give herself to him again, as she had once done. She knows she will survive whatever might happen. She is long past being a girl. She is a woman who has buried her own mother in the claggy soil of Tomnahurich cemetery and put two children on the earth. She has made a boy and so has a knowledge of what men are like before they are in any position to damage women. She knows that male viciousness is mostly just fear. From her new-found position of strength, she feels generous and indulgent to their hurtful weakness.

'Sorry, Mr Sfouf, that I haven't always been who you wanted me to be.'

He strokes her bare arm and replies, 'Yet you've been so much more.'

They feel a giddy loyalty towards what they have built up together: their disputatious, fractious, laughter-filled, silly, beautiful marriage that they love because it is so distinctly and painfully their own. They feel proud to have come this far, to have kept at it, trying again and again to understand the lunacies in each other's minds, hammering out one peace accord after another. There could have been so many reasons not to be together still. Breaking up would have been the natural, almost inevitable thing to do. It's the sticking around that is the weird and exotic achievement – and they feel a loyalty to their battle-hardened, scarred version of love.

In bed back in the room, he cherishes the marks on her stomach that their children have made, how they have torn and damaged and exhausted her with their innocent primal egoism. She notices a new undulating softness to him. It is raining heavily; the wind whistles around the battlements. When they are done, they hold each other by the window and drink a local mineral water by the light of a lamp in the yard below.

The hotel has assumed a metaphysical importance for them. The effects will not be limited to these exotic premises; they will carry the lessons in appreciation and reconciliation into the colder, plainer rooms of their daily life.

The following afternoon, Kirsten's cousin returns the children to them. Esther and William run to greet their parents in the billiard room by the reception. Esther is carrying Dobbie with her. Both parents have headaches as if they'd just stepped off a long-haul flight.

The kids complain in the strongest terms about having been abandoned like orphans and forced to sleep in a bedroom that smelt of dog. They demand explicit confirmation that this sort of trip will never happen again.

Then, as planned, the four of them go for a walk. They follow a river for a while and then ascend the foothills of Ben Nevis. After half an hour they emerge from the woods, and a landscape opens up before them that stretches out for miles in the summer sun. Far below, they can see sheep and toy-like farm buildings.

They make a base camp in a patch of heather. Esther takes off her boots and runs along a stream. She will be a woman in a few years and the story will start all over again. William tracks a trail of ants back to their nest. It is the warmest day of the year so far. Rabih lies down on the earth, spread-eagled, and follows the path of a small unthreatening cloud across the blueness.

Wanting to capture this moment, Rabih calls them to gather for a photo, then sets the camera on a rock and runs to get into the shot. He knows that perfect happiness comes in tiny, incremental units only, perhaps no more than five minutes at a time. This is what one has to take with both hands and cherish.

Struggles and conflicts will arise again soon enough: one of the children will become unhappy, Kirsten will make a short-tempered remark in response to something careless he has done, he will remember the challenges he's facing at work, he will feel scared, bored, spoilt and tired.

No one can predict the eventual fate of this photo, he knows: how it will be read in the future, what the viewer will look for in their eyes. Will it be the last photo of them all together, taken just hours before the crash on the way home, or a month before he found out about Kirsten's affair and she moved out, or the year before Esther's symptoms started? Or will it merely sit for decades in a dusty frame on a shelf in the living room, waiting to be picked up casually by William when he returns home to introduce his parents to his fiancée?

Rabih's awareness of the uncertainty makes him want to hang on to the light all the more fervently. If only for a moment, it all makes sense. He knows how to love Kirsten, how to have sufficient faith in himself and how to feel compassion for and be patient with his children. But it is all desperately fragile. He knows full well that he has no right to call himself a happy man; he is simply an ordinary human being passing through a small phase of contentment.

Very little can be made perfect, he knows that now. He has a sense of the bravery it takes to live even an utterly mediocre life like his own. To keep all of this going, to ensure his continuing status as an almost sane person, his capacity to provide for his family financially, the survival of his marriage and the flourishing of his children – these projects offer no fewer opportunities for heroism than an epic tale. He is unlikely ever to be called upon to serve his nation or to fight an enemy, but courage is required nevertheless within his circumscribed domains. The courage not to be vanquished by anxiety, not to hurt others out of frustration, not to grow too furious with the world for the perceived injuries it heedlessly inflicts, not to go crazy and somehow to manage to persevere in a more or less adequate way through the difficulties of married life – this is true courage, this is a heroism in a class all its own. And for a brief moment on the slopes of a Scottish mountain in the late-afternoon summer sun – and every now and then thereafter – Rabih Khan feels that he might, with Kirsten by his side, be strong enough for whatever life demands of him.